WATCH WHERE
THE WOLF IS GOING

STORIES
BY ANTONIO SKÁRMETA

TRANSLATED BY DONALD L. SCHMIDT
AND FEDERICO CORDOVEZ

READERS INTERNATIONAL

The stories in the present collection were first published in Spanish in various collections, including *Desnudo en el tejado* (Winner, Casa de las Américas Prize, 1969), *Tiro libre* (1973), *Novios y solitarios*, *El entusiasmo*, *No pasó nada y otros relatos* and *El ciclista del San Cristóbal*.

First published in English by Readers International Inc (USA) and Readers International (UK). Editorial inquiries to the London office at 8 Strathray Gardens, London NW3 4NY England. US/Canadian inquiries to the Subscriber Service Department, P.O.Box 959, Columbia LA 71418-0959 USA.

Cover illustration, "Everybody's Regard," by Chilean artist Jaime Azócar
Cover design by Jan Brychta
Printed and bound in Malta by Interprint Limited

Library of Congress Catalog Card Number: 91-60882

British Library Cataloguing in Publication Data
Skármeta, Antonio *1940-*
Watch where the wolf is going.
I. Title
863 [F]

ISBN 0-930523-83-0 Hardcover
ISBN 0-930523-84-9 Paperback

WATCH WHERE
THE WOLF IS GOING

by Antonio Skármeta and available
from Readers International:

I Dreamt the Snow Was Burning (novel)

Contents

Contents

The Young Man with the Story

"That's the house," Ernesto said, "a real palace. What do you think?"

I adjusted the pack on my back, and felt my entire self lapse into a kind of ecstasy, a rising temperature that came from deep within me up to my eyes, tingeing them with the force of my enthusiasm. I felt an urge to rush to the shore and run across the sand until I couldn't go on, and I could already imagine the laughter I would cause myself in doing it. "The entire blue kingdom of the earth conquered for man." There wasn't even a little bit of wind, but white sand, rocks wisely distributed, and sea and sky enough to wear you out, and my powerful, energetic throat plotted words of praise, but was mute at this moment because any word at all would stand for everything. A finger, escaped from my right hand, pointed to the incomprehensible horizon, telling at its own risk a certain story that I couldn't translate. I had a look of consternation on my face and stinging sweat on my cheeks, and Ernesto kept smiling while he looked at me, the magnanimous master of the world, asking me what did I think. He was pleasantly enjoying my veneration of the earth as he rubbed his hands, pretending to chew something, opening and closing his mouth with a slight air of self-sufficiency, always looking at me, always smiling.

"Extraordinary," I answered. "Just call me 'the King' from now on."

I talk like that, a little grandiose, what can I say.

"King of shit; by the third day you're going to need someone to talk to, you'll crave hot soup, or to see any little woman, you'll take to the highway and go back to Antofagasta."

"You don't know me," I responded, contemplating a flock of pelicans flying over a group of rocks. I'd be capable of perfectly roasting myself on a rock without a single regret. I know how to be a quiet man, God forgive me.

He grabbed an average-sized bag and deposited it on the sand.

"Here are your provisions. Canned goods and beer. Inside the railway car you'll find wine. Don't drink too much."

"Don't worry," I told him. "I won't have time."

"So, you won't have time. What do you plan to do?"

I responded with a perfectly vague, theatrical gesture; in truth, I wanted to keep secret that monologue which, to the rhythm of my breathing, was alerting me to the new land in sight, to the sudden maturity that had emerged from the tedious days spent in Santiago, near the end of my third year at the University, and which had turned my feet toward the north in a peaceful, slow trip across the plains.

"Sleep," I answered. "Like an exhausted beast. Those classes at the University make you very sleepy, you know?"

"They've always told me they keep you awake,"

Ernesto said with an astonishing cleverness.

I put my hand on his shoulder.

"Propaganda."

"But you make good grades, don't you?"

"Yes," I answered, "but that doesn't mean a thing."

"What are you going to do? Are you going to drop out of the University?"

"For a little while. I don't know. Maybe."

Ernesto scratched his head. I shrugged my shoulders and held my hand out to him.

"You'll come on Saturday?"

"For sure," he said. "Do you want me to carry the bag to the railway car for you?"

"No, leave it."

He stuck his hand in his right pocket, and then handed me the keys.

"Okay, King," he said, "have a good time."

"Don't worry," I responded.

I put the keys in my shirt pocket and picked up the provisions. Then I smiled at Ernesto and started to walk slowly toward the house. I heard the rattling of the motor and wanted him to go away quickly so I could sense the silence of the place in its fullness, and begin to hear my own voice, finally, ignorantly answering the silent questions I had been asking myself, getting the salty smell of the ocean in my nostrils. Suddenly the noise of the motor shut off, and the blast of a gun-shot shook me all over. I turned quickly toward the automobile. A hundred yards away Ernesto was gesturing to me with his arms up, indicating that he wanted me to wait for him. Instead, I took off running toward him nervously, while he rushed toward me, waving a revolver in his right hand.

When we met, he dropped down on the sand.

"What happened?" I asked. "Did you fire?"

"Yes. Take it."

I picked up the gun with my left hand. It was heavier than I had imagined.

"I almost forgot to give it to you," he said.

I looked at the revolver and switched it carefully to my other hand, making sure to keep my fingers away from the trigger.

"Is it loaded?"

"It has five bullets," he said, removing some sand that had gotten into his eye.

"What do you want me to do with it?" I asked.

I held it out for him to take.

"You keep it."

"What for? I haven't fired a single shot in my whole life."

Ernesto kept struggling with his eye. The sun was shining on his face, and with one hand he shaded himself while with the other he wiped away the tears.

"You may need it," he said. "It looks like I got some sand in my eye."

I put the revolver aside, kneeled down and took him by the head.

"Open up."

He tried to open it, but the only thing he managed was to irritate it more. When he was able to hold it open a little while, I blew on it violently several times, the very picture of a hurricane.

"Looks like it came out," he said, so that I wouldn't mess about with him any more.

He got up. I picked up the gun and held my hand out, returning it to him.

"Take this with you," I told him. "Around here the

only thing to use for target practice are pelicans. What good is it going to do me? Besides, it makes me nervous!"

"Keep it," he insisted. "This place is full of people."

I looked around sarcastically.

Beside the old railway car there was a small cabin, and a hundred yards away, another car, painted red, with a Chilean flag on a white pole.

"Yeah," I said, "there're more people here than in Glasgow, Scotland."

I turned around, following the direction of Ernesto's finger.

"Hills," I commented. "A thousand barren and beautiful hills."

"One never knows where people live," he decreed.

"Sure. What could they live on?"

"It could be that they go down to fish in the early morning, don't you think?"

I examined the gun as I held it in my right hand.

"In any case," I said, "show me how it works."

"Point somewhere."

I pointed the gun toward a rock.

"Steady it first, then pull the trigger."

"Doesn't it have a safety?"

"It's worn out."

I closed one eye and put my finger on the trigger. The detonation reverberated like a whistle in my ears, and it left my hand trembling. I missed, and a handful of sand kicked up like dust around the rock.

Ernesto laughed.

"Refine your aim," he said. "In case you have a full-scale battle, there's more ammunition in the house. If you see any Polaks, kill them."

"Okay," I said. "In your grandfather's name."

I walked the few yards that separated me from the packages, picked them up, and as I felt the car leave, continued my walk toward the house.

The first thing I did upon entering was to open the doors and all the windows to cool down the scorching interior. It was a car from the Antofagasta-Bolivia Railroad, of the same kind I had ridden in as a child, and which at one end still had two wooden seats, some coat hangers on the walls, and the luggage racks up above, stuffed now with magazines, jars, shirts and shoes, half-empty cigarette packs, empty bottles, all mixed up in admirable disorder. The car was divided by a wall made of plywood; each compartment had three cots, just like the ones soldiers use. In one corner the toilet had been retained, and in spite of someone's obvious efforts to clean them off, a mess of graffiti could still be read relatively easily. The majority of the graffiti reminded Peruvian Indians of what bastard redskins they are, and all were adorned with sketches of genitalia and delicious curves drawn above the toilet tank.

At the opposite end they had put a small table, covered by a cloth curtain, on which there were two portable kerosene stoves, and, to judge by the jars of rice and sugar, the salt, and the orange peels on the floor, that could well be a kitchen. Once I had made a complete inspection of the palace, I stretched out on each of the cots, jumping on them to test their merits, until I chose one facing the beach that had impressed me with its softness and size, and in which I could comfortably throw my six-foot frame and rest a moment, as I looked toward the ventilation louvers, whistling something or other through my teeth.

"Here I am," I said to myself, "like some shitty king peacefully cast on this bed, enjoying my exile, willing to let everything pass me by without getting upset, with three good pencils in my pocket, and with this calm comprehension that I need nothing else from the world."

"Here I am," I said afterwards under my breath, "stretched out like a clever dog hoping to recover from my fatigue, approving of the smell of sweat in my shirt, with nothing to do forever and ever, amen, slightly excited but with no desire for a woman, moving like T. S. Eliot's Chinese urn, quietly in motion, neither with nor without desire, providing a threshold for words, concentrating so that insignificant revelations become an epiphany, so that my demon will awaken and come to terms with me and we may clutch each other in an easy struggle tonight, without anything disturbing the calm surprise of the prose, while the pages advance and I, miserable wretch that I am, may petulantly rub my hand across my nose, as if I knew myself to be the filthy master of the world, yelling at the top of my lungs just from the joy of being, with no wind capable of knocking me off my steed, and too free to start writing like a maniac just now.

"Let's see what the beach has to offer," I said getting up, "and don't let anything bother you, unless you feel like being bothered, and in that case, don't let anything calm you down, brother."

I put my hand over my eyes like a visor, and, looking at the sun, I estimated the time of day. It looked like it was around five in the afternoon, so I would still have sunlight for a good while. I walked, stretching myself and yawning, until I was a few yards from the water's edge, and, throwing off my clothes, I stretched out naked on the sand, immediately feeling the sun's warmth on my face and belly. I had put my rolled up shirt under my neck, so I was peacefully relaxing in total comfort. With my eyes barely open I watched the heavy beating of the pelicans' wings as they circled an area of water that seemed to be stocked with sardines, and I saw them suddenly dive beak-first, plunging into the sea, and then emerge toward the air, drenched, with fish grasped firmly in their beak. There were about thirty of these huge birds flying around, and, enhanced by the tranquility of the ocean, the sound of their wings, beating against the calm, brilliant atmosphere, could be heard intensely, like a kind of dry reverberation resembling music. I also picked out other smaller birds whose name I didn't know that were cutting through the air way up high, but their entire motion was harmonious, and they didn't seem to be looking for food or attempting to catch fish, nor did they seem to be headed for any particular place either, since the only thing they were doing was to circle in the same place, sometimes in a line, or in a group of four. It could have been that the only thing they wanted was just to be there flying, just because it was good for them, since that was their life, holding themselves suspended in the air, gliding after having flapped enough to achieve that serene transport on their own, perhaps joyous at simply being useless birds in flight, way up high, like a black spot stretching out against the color of the sky, segmenting the sun, slicing it into hundreds of tiny suns, snatching from it, as I imagined, its only depth, carrying off its radiance grasped in their beaks, sliding it over their black plumage, shaking it with their pointed heads, and reintegrating it into the air, so as to divide the air, in turn, and freely place themselves in space.

"This is what I am," I said, caressing my belly without ceasing to watch the birds, imbued by their oscillations, disengaged from my name and from the world, quietly withdrawn, trapping myself. "This is what I am. Space. I begin here, and at the tip of the dirty, twisted toes of my feet I end. And this is what is given to me, and now I can begin to be thankful for it."

I rubbed my hand across my burning face, hard to the touch, with a few grains of sand scratching my cheeks, and attempted to give thanks for my space in the first idiom that came into my head.

The first thing I said was a kind of prayer, mixing in the Lord's Prayer with the odes of Neruda and with some poems I had written in my childhood, all peppered with obscenities that I threw in just to shake up the act of thanksgiving, as if I thought that if anyone were to hear them, at least they wouldn't take me for a prude or a conventional poet. Then it occurred to me that it would be just the right thing to ask for a guarantee that my space would be preserved inviolate, except, that is, for women, should it occur to any of them to violate it, but not by death nor plagues nor any similar nastiness. The sun began softly to annoy me, so I turned over on my stomach, resting my face on the right side, and, looking just at the nearest portion of sand, I kept on threading together my discourse, taking care to make it sound honorable and persuasive.

Immediately, emboldened by my prayer and inclined toward ambition by the sound of my words, which were a sentence murmured into the ear of the female stretched out at my side, the only one, the chosen one, and inclined also by the sunshine that perched on my back side, and by the hot sand pressing against my belly, I raised my voice in protest at not having more than I had, in rebellion against time, taunting it about its honest destruction, arguing against the law of gravity, which doesn't carry you to the stars when you lightly push yourself off a rock with a certain anxiety to go far, as far as possible. I argued against the word "possible," calling for its eradication from the dictionary, protesting against the absurd usurpation that will occur one day thanks to the air that I will magnanimously return to the universe with hope every time I inhale, the same bellicose air that I was now hurling like stones against the sand, making it jump, making it rise, dislodging it from its natural order. Suddenly, in the face of that sort of pain, the only thing left was heredity: to see yourself converted into a shrieking, wet thing that would be painful just to look at, that would testify before you right there where your body declares its retreat that he is present, on your turf, thanks to your strenuous apprenticeship in the labors of the world, in all its absurd pain and joy, that would watch you with your few pounds of weight, denouncing you, for it is you there, better than you used to be, or, otherwise, just right there, but betrayed definitively, with him turned about, confronting you, not accepting you, denying the world without a single word, silently dispatching priest and mystery to hell itself, freely choosing his death, ceasing to breathe on the night of his birth, or retreating at twenty years of age after having concluded his lesson at the doorstep of a brothel, without a gesture, without a lie, with quiet sarcasm, thinking about faith, denying sentiment, shaking his head, retracting his life like a feather settled on his hair: just as light or bothersome as that; or years later, in the distance, watching him myself through a window that opens onto the beach, stretched out on the sand, asking himself the same questions. I will see him touching his genitals, thinking about himself, testing the answer by getting the woman who listens at his side pregnant, or perhaps remaining quiet, and then perhaps I'll know my own name and be able to go to sleep in my bed leaving the windows open so the sea breeze can saturate my wrinkles, carve and exhaust them in order for me to keep silent with the taste of fermented salt on my cheeks.

With my toes and fingers I took to scratching in the sand while I flexed my knees and elbows, sensing the fine shower of sand beating against my neck, and with the motion of nodding "no" I dragged my forehead in the sand, marking a kind of semicircle. I was speeding up all these movements involuntarily, without intending to, until it seemed like all the heat in the world was being turned over to me, and like there was a pile of coal stacking up with intermittent movements in my brain, in my thighs, and in my spine, especially. I clung to the earth, squeezing a conch shell in my right hand, and, keeping still, I let myself circulate freely through my veins and then emerge violently toward the rest of space, feeling the humid contact on my stomach, chest and neck, panting heavily, with my hands extended now, as if I were crucified, without ceasing to dig in the sand with my forehead, holding my eyes firmly closed, and smiling.

When everything had passed, I stayed a second longer in the same position contemplating the event, waiting for my breathing to return to normal, entwining the hair on my chest. Once things were in order, yawning with satisfaction, I turned over. I ended up on my back, and with the sudden opening of my eyes and the direct light of the sun beating down on them, which I hadn't seen in at least half an hour, I was blinded and forced to close them for a moment. I wiped away the tears with the palms of my hands, and when I was finally able to look toward the beach, I couldn't resist stretching, to show the state of satisfaction growing inside me as I contemplated the sea, which was absolutely serene now, except for the glistening of the sun across the water, which produced a kind of barely perceptible movement. The birds were motionless on the rocks, scanning the horizon with their beaks, squawking noisily, as if involved in an argument over the remoteness that the world was arranging in those shades of blue which the sun was beginning to sneak into.

On entering the water, the first thing I did was stand submerged knee-deep, while I cleaned my stomach and chest with my right hand, and flicked refreshing drops of water on my face with my fingers. I took water in my hand, raised it over my head, and then let it fall on my hair as if baptizing myself, and when I said my name, Antonio, I noticed that it didn't seem alien to me, that I obeyed myself if I used it, and the whole time I stood there throwing water on my head and repeating my name, I saw an image of myself in which I was repeating my name and throwing water on my head. The only thing was that I, the one doing the imagining, was looking seriously toward the horizon, with sort of a headache that was starting to annoy me, while the imaginary one seemed, instead, to be laughing at everything, and it occurred to me that he had just taken off his coat with tails, had arranged his trousers on sand perfumed with lavender, and without picking up the chips won at the Casino, had waded into the sea, to ask undramatically, indeed with joy, what his name on this earth was.

I knew that by swimming I could habituate my body to the temperature of the water, so when I came up from my first dive, I started flailing my arms rapidly, splashing noisily, and turned about with no fixed direction, doing all kinds of violent maneuvers. When I felt myself to be master of the sea, I swam slowly toward a big rock sticking up a hundred yards away, using harmonious, balanced strokes, spitting out to the sides the salt water that was getting into my half-open mouth, with my eyes closed, opening them only occasionally to assure myself I was still headed in a straight line. I was concerned about the contrast between my painful head and the magnificent state of internal force in the rest of my body, its comfortable semi-tension, the clarity with which my lungs were working the air as I swam, and the dialogue I had engaged with the ocean. While I waved my arms, I pushed it away, turning it back toward shore like a conqueror sighting new lands.

As soon as I got to the rock, I stood up on it and in a sing-song voice said out loud the names of everything around there, repeating the ones I liked best, such as mountain, shore, sea gull, pelican, truth, and others like them, until I said "crab," even though there wasn't a single one nearby. I said it just to make an ass of myself, because I liked the word, or maybe because, in fact, I wanted a crab to appear, but I hadn't stopped saying the word when just next to my right foot one emerged. Then I remembered a certain book, smiled ironically as I bent over to pick it up, and although my lips, my eyes and my entire body were watching the crab kick, somehow I knew that all the vanity in the world together with that of Ecclesiastes, and all the great vanity that one day must wisely come had gotten into me right down to my most concealed bones, because when I was smiling ironically at the crab, somehow I knew I was looking upward.

I ran the crab through with a wooden stick I found floating nearby, and began my return to the beach, swimming slowly, with the pierced crab following the ups and downs of my right arm carrying it, still struggling to live, as if invigorated by the sudden dips into the water caused by my strokes.

Without drying off, I put my clothes on and walked toward the railway car. It was starting to get dark and my headache, which had made its presence known some time ago, got more penetrating. My lips felt dry, and inside my head images were appearing as if they had been placed under the light of flashing orange reflectors, and it was much more painful if I closed my eyes. Before reaching the door to the house, I felt my first chill. I put my hand on my forehead, to confirm if I had a fever, but my hand felt as hot as my head. I went into the house cursing my bad luck, buttoning my shirt and shaking my body to ward off that sort of icy current that was making it quiver every few moments. And I got madder still when I saw the open notebooks on the table, and on their blank pages the three highly polished and sharpened pencils. My urge to write grew, but rabidly, annoying me, just as if I had grabbed a club to kill a pesky gnat. I closed the notebooks, stretched out on the bed and decided simply to await the night, watching through the window until it became absolutely dark. I would first watch the failing light of dusk, and later, watch the darkness, without talking to myself, blanking out my mind so that no image would awaken me and trouble me. With my eyes half open I would close off the pathways to my nerves, and, looking into the distance, I would die provisionally in order to rest. I knew that as soon as I dropped my guard, as soon as the first thing took form in my heart, I would stand up, open the notebook and for eight hours I would write down all the hate and frustration that a youngster at twenty years of age can have accumulated against the world, filling the pages with that weepy slop, just to awaken on the beach, imbecilic and dirty, dead tired, knowing positively that man is beyond all that, and, in that way, I would be denying the world, disintegrating the mysterious emotion that both unites and disarranges everything. When everything was dark, except for the starry sky, and for the white fringe of foam sprung from the ebb tide at the water's edge, I couldn't keep my eyes open, nor control my fever any longer. My head began to fail me; my body felt weak and sweaty, and I slid between the blankets half asleep. In spite of the fever, I managed to sleep a couple of hours without a single image bothering me.

What woke me up suddenly was voices. I kept still, fixing my attention on the sound. With my eyes wide open I tried to see in the room. The night was clear and everything seemed calm. I straightened up a little to see out the window, but when I was about to show my face in the frame, I threw myself back, shivering. The voices could no longer be heard, and it occurred to me that it could have been just my imagination. After all, I had got a first-class sunburn, so what could be strange about my hearing non-existent voices? In bed, with my hands clinging to the edges, I stayed ready to jump up if I saw anyone come in, throw myself on him, or maybe escape through the window and run the mile and a half to the highway.

"Vagrants," I thought. "Miners fired from Chuqui-camata, or from the saltpeter beds themselves. Who else could it be? Who else would come through here, miles from the nearest civilization, at midnight?"

Tossing around on the bed I threw out all suppositions, and, covered up to my ears, I tried to get back to sleep. If what I wanted was to be alone, I told myself, then I had to withstand anxiety and learn not to fear the night, but instead to live off the darkness and to savor its opaque sap, in the same way I got tepid nourishment from the light of day.

The silence calmed me. With my head placed under the bedspread, I kept my concentration on the sound of the night, the motion of the sea, and, occasionally, very much in the distance, only percept-ible by one who was very attentive, the horns of the trucks that were coming back from Chuquicamata, taking advantage of the cool of the night. I put one hand between my legs, and bending my knees, I hunched my back forward and very slowly whispered a jazz tune. Always hanging on the noises outside, I would interrupt the song from time to time, and although I couldn't remember many of the lyrics, I would continue, inventing the words I needed to finish the melodic phrases. I don't know if the theme was sad, one of those by Chet Baker, or if the fever produced it, or if the most hopeful of stories was serenely beginning to break apart inside me, but what is certain is that tears began to cover my face, concentrating the fever in my corneas. Bursting forth unabated, the tears rolled down my chin and fell on my neck. When I inhaled forcefully, as if sighing, the air penetrating me was colder, and I felt it convulse in my guts. It wasn't because of the sounds I had heard before. Nor the darkness. Nor was it the absolute silence of the moment, save for my intermittent song, which I didn't stop singing, as if that melody would protect me, cradle me snugly, and warm the thoughts that were disturbing me.

All of what was there, curled up, folded up all over me, boiling at 110°F beneath the luminous night sky, all that vain, shivering garbage which, with chin thrust out and a gesture of pride, I called "I," as I inflated the word, repeating it while I jumped on the ground until my cheeks flopped loosely. It was all that marvelous blue, that testimonial blue, the love held in, the smile, all the prose and all the bragging, I had them all there, clinging to my guts like the crab that was going to make a good breakfast for me. Those were all inert things feeding on my fear, feeding from the udders of that old heavy cow I had suddenly become, lacking all agility or grace, feeling pain every time I stretched a muscle, and, with still more fear at each creak of the cot, each gust of breeze over the papers in the room. Those were the things that were separating me still further from the rest of the world, handing me over to a profound mystery; only the mystery wasn't benign, because what it most seemed like was a slow, morbid illness that savored the being it was devouring, possessing it as if standing over the bed, as if from within, or from the air tasting of salt, and from within what didn't yet exist, and from within provincial Sunday afternoons, when I would gaze at the dust of the deserted sidewalks, when that flavor had already appeared in the sweat under white shirt collars.

For a second I shook my head energetically, spit on my fingers and rubbed them over my eyelids to refresh them, trying once more to keep still so that not a single image could reattach me to fear. I listened. There were, in fact, no sounds.

But suddenly, with unmistakable clarity, someone laughed, in what sounded like a grave, hoarse rattle, and that laugh was followed by another that was weak, almost feminine. I calculated where they must be coming from. They seemed to be on the right side of the car, probably leaning against the wall that faced the hill. I was tense. The laughter sounded again, weaker now, as if it were a final comment on the previous laughter. A silence followed. There was a noise in the back window, near the kitchen, that made me sit up and scrutinize the back of the house. Then a leg appeared, hanging there for a moment, and soon the other one appeared, while the rest of the body struggled to get in, impelled by the two arms braced on the upper part of the window frame. I groped for the revolver on the bedspread lying on the floor where I had thrown my trousers before going to bed. I stuck my hand in the pocket, and was relieved to touch the cold metal of the gun. I switched it to my right hand, raised it to eye level, and aimed it at the legs of the man who was still at the window, gesturing at someone to come closer, while at the same time he was moving his head from side to side as if to assure himself that no one was watching. He even looked toward where I was, but because he hadn't yet adjusted to the darkness inside, and because the only thing moving was my arm with the revolver, he didn't spot me. Before pulling the trigger, I made a gesture like someone pausing a moment to reflect. It was a motion like a sharp breath that calmed me unexpectedly, that cooled me off, took away my fever, as if I had suddenly vomited it up.

"I'm nuts," I thought, "absolutely nuts."

I lowered the gun, and in the moment when the second guy was beginning to come through the window, I stood up firmly on my bare feet, and let loose a brief, shrieking yell.

"Who goes there!" I shouted, backing up. Instinctively I raised the gun.

The one who was coming in retreated noisily, dropping to the sand at a signal from the right hand of the one already inside.

Wrinkling my forehead I tried to see clearly what the man was doing by that dark part of the wall. First, always keeping the gun raised, I withstood the silence, with something that wasn't precisely patience, but a bit later, the fact that he didn't move, and that I couldn't even hear him breathe started to get me agitated, and as I moved forward a little, I spoke to him.

"What are you doing here?" I said. "What do you want?"

There was perfect silence.

"What are you doing?" I repeated. "I'm armed and aiming at you. I can see you perfectly."

I could feel the revolver wet from the sweat of my

hand. I moved my index finger over the trigger, rubbing it to dry it.

"Well," I continued, adding a note of forcefulness to the fake serenity with which I had been speaking, "I'm not going to stand here all night waiting for you to answer. If you don't answer, I'm going to fire, understand? I'm armed; I can see you, right?"

I hadn't stopped speaking when I saw the form move, breaking its motionlessness with a short jump. It seemed to come in my direction, and dodging to the side, I pulled the trigger twice, and ended up sitting on the bed from the revolver's kick. Once again that vibration I had felt in the morning hung in the air. The flashes blinded me for a second, and as I stood up, it seemed that I could make out the man near the window.

"Don't fire again!" he said. "Please!"

I rubbed my hand over my forehead.

"How are you? Did I wound you?"

"It doesn't look like it," he said lisping.

"I didn't shoot at your body," I bragged, just in case something might happen.

"Thanks," he said. "We're honest people. Don't worry, sir."

"Call your friend," I ordered.

He whistled at him through the window.

"He's my son. He's only a boy."

I looked outside.

"Just come on in, Pedro. The gentleman thought we were burglars, and that's why he fired. Don't be scared. Just come on in."

I put the revolver aside and lit a candle.

As I was twisting the flame around to drop some wax where I could set the candle, I focused on the man's traits, his stocky build, his three-day beard, his green working clothes, and then, when he came in, I focused on the kid, bundled up in a worn-out leather jacket, and a pair of shorts.

On the table I discovered a couple of aspirins, which I tossed into my mouth, and began sucking on them loudly.

"Well, what is it you want?" I asked.

The two looked at each other.

"We're just passing through, sir. To Antofagasta," the man added. "We thought there was no one here, so that's why we tried to get in."

"We're tired," the boy said, rubbing the back of his hand over his eyes. "We wanted a place to sleep."

"A little bed, right, Pedro?"

"Of course."

"We knew there were beds in these houses. They told us that, right, Pedro?"

The child nodded.

At that moment I was more ashamed than the devil.

"Lie down there," I said, pointing to two beds in the other room.

I went over to their side and picked up a demijohn.

"Here's some wine, in case you're thirsty."

"Don't bother, sir."

I handed them my bag of provisions and told them to take something to eat.

"From the scare," I told them, "my head aches. Good night."

"Good night. Thanks. Why did you go to all the bother, sir? We're gonna stay here real quiet. Now, go to bed, Pedro."

I went back to my cot, calmed, ashamed, and

before getting in bed I picked up the ammunition box and put it on the floor within reach. Stretched out on the bed, playing with the unloaded revolver, spinning it in my right hand, I thought about the world and people; I thought about all those who live in cities and about those who go from city to city, from country to country, from planet to planet, as if there were some place where things were going to be better, as if there were some place you could take off your shoes, without ever having to fear again, balanced in your destiny, steering it with your hand, directly touching its value and charm in the warm pulse of hope, and say here's where I'll stay and nothing will move me. And I need nothing to stay here; I fear no one, and I can stop loving no one, and I can look with disdain on anyone I choose; and there will be creation here; and much can be learned by watching the sea. This time, stretched out on the bed, I was picking up the bullets one by one and placing them in the round chambers of the gun, until I finished loading it. I left the gun on the floor, and turning my face to the wall, I closed my eyes and quickly fell asleep.

When I awoke I looked through the window and what was out there was nothing other than a bright, warm day. It looked to be about ten in the morning. I was on my feet in one leap; and then, dressed, I went to the other compartment to see my guests. The beds were unmade but there was no sign of either of the two. I took the revolver and the box, and went outside. I stepped on the warm sand, and, using my hands like blinders, I looked for them all along the beach. I could make them out near a group of rocks, making strange, contorted motions on the sand, as if they were digging with their feet. As I approached, I saw that they were gathering something and putting it in a wooden box. Also, beside the box I could make out the demijohn of wine and a bucket. They gestured jubilantly when they saw me coming. When I was once at their side, the man came up and handed me a kind of shellfish, palpitating.

"Help yourself," he told me. "They're razor clams."

I picked it up and chewed on it, noting its flavor.

"Now, show me how you find them," I said.

"They're buried in the wet sand. Move you're foot and you'll see."

That's what I did and I wasn't long in finding one, and it smelled very good.

We spent a long time digging, and once we had filled the box we sat on the boulders; and on the clams we put lemon, which my guests had brought; we began to eat, and between one clam and another, we tossed down swigs of wine, at first brief and refreshing, and then long and somniferous, until the three of us were half drunk. Still thirsty, we sent Pedro back to the house to get another demijohn, and when he got back, we drank that one too, and continued digging in the sand and eating clams until I thought I would burst.

I leaned against a wall and closed my eyes while the world did demented pirouettes and the sea looked red or orange, or almost yellow. I opened my eyes and discovered that my two companions were sleeping, covered by the sand in which they had wallowed. Then I remembered my headache, but what I felt was so sweet that it was hard to think that at one time I could have had a headache. I picked up the revolver, aimed at the horizon and fired. I kept listening to the echo for a few seconds, and then I aimed at the horizon

again and pulled the trigger. Afterwards, I fired off
the rest of the bullets without stopping to listen to the
sound, and, as loud as I could, I sang one of those
background tunes they play in cowboy movies.

Then I picked up the ammunition box, loaded the
revolver and fired at the sky, at the house, breaking
two windows, at the driftwood floating along the
shore, at the hills, at a boat passing in the distance, at
everything in me that I wished would die. When I had
used up the ammunition, and the hammer went click,
and I noticed my burning hand and my upset stomach,
I got up, shook my two companions without managing
to wake them up, headed for the house, undressing as
I went, until I stood before the bed, and, smiling, I
dropped into it to wait for the night to come, free of
all bonds, naked like the birds, falling into sleep,
sinking into a sweet abyss, thinking, as I was losing
consciousness totally, about the story I would
write that night.

The Cyclist from San Cristóbal

> *...and I humbled myself so much*
> *that I went as high as high could be,*
> *and then my prey I could reach.*
>
> San Juan de la Cruz

And what's more, it was my birthday. From the balcony on Alameda Avenue I saw that Russian Sputnik the newspapers were always talking about creep across the sky. But I didn't drink a drop because the next day was the first hill-climb of the season and my mother was sick in a room that wasn't much bigger than a closet. The only thing I had left to do was lie on the floor and peddle with my feet in the air to toughen up my muscles so I could hit the pedals tomorrow with that style of mine they wrote about in *Estadio*. While my mama was floating in fever, I began to wander through the hallways eating the cakes Aunt Margarita had given me, crumb by crumb, diligently sorting out the pieces of candied fruit with the tip of my tongue and spitting them out the side of my mouth, making a real mess. My old man came out every little while to taste the punch, and every time he would spend five minutes stirring it, then he would sigh, and with his fingers would pick at the chunks of peach floating like shipwrecks in the mixture of cheap white wine, brandy, Orange Crush and mineral water.

Both of us needed something to hurry the night along and bring the morning. I decided to interrupt my exercises and polish my shoes; my old man was leafing through the phone book, probably with the idea of calling an ambulance. The sky was clear, the night was very warm, and, while she was half asleep, Mama would say, "I'm burning up," just loud enough for us to hear her through the open doorway.

But that was a night to make your hair stand on end, and the son-of-a-bitch wouldn't let up even for a little bit. Looking at each star was just like counting cactuses in the desert, like biting your nails until they bleed, like reading Dostoevsky. Then Dad would go into the room and repeat the same incredible arguments in my mother's ear, that the injection would bring down her fever, that the sky was already starting to get light, that the doctor was going to come by early in the morning before he went off fishing in Cartagena.

Finally, we tried to play tricks on the darkness. We took advantage of a milky quality the sky has in the wee hours, and tried to confuse it with the light of dawn (with a little encouragement I could have even made out the crowing of a rooster right there in the center of downtown).

It could have been any time between three and four o'clock when I went into the kitchen to make breakfast. As if they were co-ordinated, the whistling of the teapot and my mother's yelling got louder and louder. Dad appeared in the doorway.

"I can't make myself go in," he said.

He looked fat and pale, and his shirt was simply dripping. We could hear Mama saying: "Get the doctor."

"He said he'd come by first thing in the morning," my old man repeated for the fifth time.

I had become fascinated with the way the kettle lid

was jumping around, bounced by the steam.

"She's going to die," I said.

Dad started to pat pockets all over his body. A sign that he wanted to smoke. Now it would cost him a hell of an effort to find the cigarettes, next the same thing would happen with the matches, and then I would have to light it for him off the gas stove.

"You think so?"

I raised my eyebrows this much and sighed.

"Hand me your cigarette so I can light it for you."

As I got close to the flame, it confused me when I noticed that the fire didn't hurt my nose like all the other times. I handed the cigarette to my father, without turning my head, and consciously put my little finger over the small flame. It was like nothing. I thought: This finger has died on me or something, but you can't think about the death of a finger without laughing a little, so I held out my whole palm, and this time I touched the gas outlet with my finger tips, each one of its holes, stirring around at the very roots of the flames. Dad wandered from one end of the hallway to the other, taking care to drop ashes on his collar and to get bits of tobacco all over his moustache. I took advantage of the opportunity to push the thing a little further, and put my wrists on to toast, and then my elbows, and then all my fingers again. I turned the gas off, spat on my hands, which felt dry, and took the basket with the stale bread, the jar of jelly and a brand new package of butter to the dining room.

When Dad sat down at the table, I must have started to cry. With his neck bent over, he buried his gaze in his black coffee as if all the resignation on earth were concentrated there. Then he said something I couldn't hear, because he seemed to be carrying on an incredulous dialogue with some intimate part of his body, a kidney maybe, or a thighbone. Then he put his hand in his open shirt, and ran his fingers through the tangled mesh of hair on his chest. On the table there was a basket of slightly bruised plums, apricots and peaches. For a moment the fruit just sat there cradled, virgin, and I started to stare at the wall like I was watching a movie or something. Finally I grabbed a nectarine and rubbed it on my collar until I got a pretty passable shine on it. Just like it was catching, my old man picked up a plum.

"Your mother's going to die," he said.

I rubbed my neck hard. Now I was rolling around the fact I hadn't got burned. With my tongue I licked off the seed, and with my hands I started to push the crumbs together on the table, making little piles out of them, and then with my finger I flicked them between the cup and the bread basket. At the same moment I was pushing the seed against my cheek bone, and imagining I had a huge swelling around a molar, I put a serious expression on my face and thought I had discovered the reason I had become incombustible - if you can say that. The whole thing wasn't very clear yet, but I had the same evidence that leads to a forecast of rain, like when the birds take shelter in the middle of the day: If Mama was going to die, I'd have to emigrate from the planet, too. The thing with the fire was like a synopsis of a horror film, or maybe it was just some blah-blah of mine, and the only thing that was happening was that so many trips to the movies had corrupted me.

I looked at Dad, and just as I was going to tell him

about it, he squeezed his chubby palms together in front of his eyes until the space between them was impenetrable.

"She's going to live," I said. "Fever is scary."

"It's like the body's defense."

I cleared my throat.

"If I win the race we'll have money. We could put her in a decent clinic."

"If by chance she doesn't die."

I spat the seed, which I had polished with so much sucking, over my shoulder. The old man convinced himself to take a bite out of a pretty tasty looking peach. We heard Mama complain in her room, this time without words. I finished off my coffee in three gulps, almost comforted by the fact that it hurt my mouth. I stuck a French roll in my pocket, and, as I was getting up, the squadron of crumbs moved over to freshen up in something like a puddle of wine, which was fresh only in appearance, because since Mama had been in bed, stains on the table cloth lasted a month, pleading under their breath.

I adopted a casual tone to say good-bye, halfway like a Gringo, you might say.

"I'm leaving."

As his only response, Dad turned his head and surveyed the night.

"What time's the race?" he asked, sipping a little coffee. I felt like a pig, and not precisely like one of those nice guys who appear in the comics.

"At nine. I'm going to go warm up a little."

I took the clips for my trousers out of my pocket, and grabbed my equipment bag. Simultaneously I was humming a tune by the Beatles, one of those psychedelic ones.

"Maybe you ought to get a little sleep," Dad suggested. "It's already been two nights that..."

"I feel fine," I said, heading toward the door.

"Okay, then."

"Don't let your coffee get cold."

I closed the door as sweetly as if I were kissing a chick, and then I opened the lock on my bike, pulling it off the bars of the balcony railing. I stuck it under my armpit, and, without waiting on the elevator, I ran down the four flights to the street. I stood there a minute, caressing the tires without knowing which way to go, while now there really was an early morning breeze blowing slowly, a little cold.

I got on, and with one push on the pedals I got out to the curb and started along Alameda Avenue to Bulnes Plaza, where I cruised around the circular rim of the fountain. Then I turned left to Negro Tobar's cabaret and hung around under the awning to listen to the music coming from the cellar. What was getting in the way was not being able to smoke, not destroying the image of the perfect athlete that our coach had drummed into our heads. Whenever I showed up with tobacco on my breath, he would smell my tongue, and you're outta here. But most of all, I was like a stranger in the early Santiago morning. I might have been the only jerk in Santiago whose mother was dying, the absolutely only kid in the galaxy who hadn't figured out how to get himself a chick to brighten up partyless Saturday nights, definitely the only creature who cried when somebody told him sad stories. And suddenly I placed the quartet's song, as Lucho Aranguiz's trumpet was blowing that phrase, "*I can't give you anything but love, Baby; that's the only thing I've plenty of, Baby.*" Two couples walked past in

silence, like ashes scattering in the wake of passing
schoolkids, and there was something gloomy and
unforgettable in the murmur of the corner fire
hydrant. The milkman's wagon seemed to emerge
from the silvery sea of the fountain's pool, slowly, in
spite of his spirited horses, and the wind was pushing
along cigarette and popsicle wrappers. The drummer
was dragging out his theme like a long cord with
nothing tied to the end of it - *sha-sha-da-da* - and a
sweaty, drunk young man came out of the cellar to
wipe his nose, with his eyes bleary and bloodshot from
the smoke, the knot on his tie dislocated, and his hair
bunched up at his temples. The orchestra started into
a sophisticated tango, always the same, one is always
searching, full of hope, and at any moment the
buildings on Bulnes Avenue could fall down dead, and
the wind could blow even harder, and it would make
sailboats, barges and masts out of the scaffolding, it
would make barrels of alcohol from the modern
heaters, it would change doors into sea gulls, parquets
into foam, radios and irons into fish, lovers' beds
would burst into flame, tuxedos, underwear and
bracelets would be crabs, shellfish, and sand, and the
hurricane would give to each face what belongs to it: a
mask to the aged, broken laughter to the schoolboy,
and to the young virgin, the sweetest pollen. All of
them knocked over by the clouds, all of them smashed
against the planets, emptying themselves in death, and
me among them, pedalling a hurricane with my
bicycle, saying don't die Mama, me singing *Lucy in the
Sky with Diamonds*, and the cops with their useless
whips lashing imaginary colts, straddling the wind,
flailed by parks as high as kites, by statues; and me
reciting the stanzas I had most recently learned in

Spanish class, almost lethargically, sketching something pornographic in Aguilera's notebook, swiping
Kojman's lunch, sticking a pencil in Skinny Leiva's
ass; me reciting, and the young man tightened his belt
with the same restraint that someone thirsty for
tenderness uses to abandon a lover's bed, and all of a
sudden I was singing frivolously, oblivious to the
words, as if each song were only a rain shower before
the morning dew. Then I went stumbling down the
stairs, and Luchito Aranguiz was doing a solo on the
trumpet, beginning to step up the tempo, and
everything turned to jazz, and when I tried to seek out
a little of the early morning air to cool off my palate,
my throat, the fever that was breaking out between
my belly and my liver, my head banged against the
wall, violently, noisily. I was stunned, and dug around
in my pockets, took out a cigarette pack and smoked
avidly, greedily, while I was sliding down the wall until
I put my body on the floor tiles. Then I crossed my
hands and fell devoutly asleep.

I was awakened by the drums, batons and trumpets
of some group that was marching around the well of
Santiago, not heading for war at all, but decked out as
if for a celebration. All I had to do was get on my bike
and speed down a couple of blocks to witness the
resurrection of ice cream cone makers, of pitiful old
women, of peanut vendors, and of beardless adoles-
cents wearing shirts and boots in the latest style. If the
clock on the church of San Francisco wasn't lying this
time, I had exactly seven minutes left to get to the
starting line at the base of San Cristóbal hill.
Although my body was racked by cramps, I hadn't lost
my precise aim for the pedal's rubber. And besides,
there was a huge sun shining, and the sidewalks

looked almost deserted.

When I crossed the Pío Nono bridge, things began to pick up. I noticed that the competitors warming up along the base of the hill were flattering me with sidelong glances. I was able to make out Lopez, from the Audax team, blowing his nose, Ferruto, from the Green team, pumping up a tire, and the guys on my team listening to our coach's instructions.

When I joined the group, they gave me a look of disapproval, but they didn't light into me. I took advantage of the opportunity to come on like a prima donna.

"Do I have time to make a phone call?" I asked.

The coach pointed to the dressing room.

"Go get dressed."

I gave my bike to the handler.

"It's urgent," I explained. "I need to call home."

"What for?"

But before I could explain it to him I imagined myself in the bar across the street surrounded by kids, characters fit for the zoo, and pale drunks, dialling my home number to ask my dad...what? Did Mama die? Did the doctor come by the house? How's she doing?

"It's not important," I responded. "I'll go get dressed." I dove into the tent and resolutely got undressed. When I was naked, I proceeded to claw at my thighs, and then at my calves and ankles until I felt my body respond. I squeezed my abdomen tight with the elastic belt, and then covered all the red marks made by my fingernails with my socks. While I was adjusting my racing suit, using its elastic band to hold my shirt, I realized I was going to win the race. Having spent a sleepless night, with my throat so dry it was cracked and with a bitter taste in my mouth, with my legs as stiff as a mule's, I was going to win the race. I was going to win it against the coach, against Lopez, against Ferruto, against my own team mates, my father, my classmates and my teachers, my own bones, my head, my belly, my dissipation, my own and my mother's death, against the president of the country, against Russia and the United States, the bees, fish, birds, pollen; I was going to win it against the universe.

I grabbed an elastic bandage and double-wrapped the instep, bottom and ankle of each foot. When I had them wrapped up like a fist, the only thing sticking out were my ten fleshy, aggressive, flexible toes.

I came out of the tent. "I'm an animal," I thought, when the judge raised his pistol, "I'm going to win this race because I have claws and hooves on each foot. I heard the pistol shot and with two sharp, chopping pushes on the pedals I hit the first rise, in the lead. As soon as the slope eased, I just let the sun melt on the back of my neck. I didn't have to look very far back to find Pizarnick, from the Ferroviario team, stuck to my ass. I felt sorry for the boy, for his team, and for his coach, who had told him, "If he takes the lead, stick to him as long as you can, calm and smart, understand?" because if I wanted to, right there I could set a pace that would have that boy puking in less than five minutes, with his lungs turned inside out, failed, incredulous. In the first curve the sun disappeared, and I raised my head toward the statue of the Virgin at the top of the hill, and she looked sweetly aloof, incorruptible. I decided to play it smart, and by abruptly slowing the rhythm of my pedalling, I let Pizarnick take the lead. But the kid was riding with the Bible in his saddle-bag: he slacked off until he was even with me, and a blond kid from Stade Français strongly took the lead. I turned my head to the left and smiled at Pizarnick.

"Who's he?" I asked him.

The boy didn't look back at me.

"What?" he panted.

"Who's that?" I repeated. "The one who passed us."

He didn't seem to have noticed that we were a few yards back. "I don't know him," he said. "Did you see what make of bike it was?"

"A Legnano," I responded. "What are you thinking about?"

But this time I didn't get an answer. I realized that the whole time he had been thinking about whether he should catch up to the new leader now that I had given up the lead. If he had only asked me, I would have clued him in; too bad his Bible wasn't a walkie-talkie. A little steeper hill, and see ya later alligator. He peddled and kicked until he caught up with the blond, and in near desperation he looked back to check the distance. I looked to the sides for another competitor to talk with, but I was alone about twenty yards from the lead pack, and the rest of my rivals were just getting their noses around the curve. I grabbed at my pounding heart with the fingers of one hand, and was holding on to the middle of the handlebar with the other one by itself. How could I be so alone all of a sudden! Where was the blond, and Pizarnick? And González, and the guys from my club, and the ones from Audax Italiano? Why was I starting to run out of air, why was the sky getting so crushingly overcast above the roofs of Santiago? Why was sweat hurting my eyelids, filling my eyes and making everything blurry? My heart wasn't beating that hard just to get blood to my legs, nor to burn my ears, nor to press my ass harder against the saddle and put more kick into each push. That heart of mine was betraying me, it was rebelling against the slope, banging blood through my nose, fogging up my eyes, shaking my arteries, bouncing on my diaphragm, leaving me tied perfectly to an anchor, with my body like a rope, graceless, in submission.

"Pizarnick!" I shouted. "Stop, dammit, I'm dying!"

But my words just flowed back and forth between my temples, between my upper and lower teeth, between my salivary glands and carotid arteries. My words were a perfect circle of flesh: I had never said anything. I had never talked with anyone on earth. I had spent the whole time repeating an image in shop windows, in mirrors, in winter puddles, in girls' eyes, darkened by thick make-up. And maybe now - pedalling and pedalling, step by step, gasping and gasping - that same silence was coming over Mama - and I was going up and up, and down and down - the same blue death you get from asphyxia - struck and broken, struck and broken - death of dirty noses and a gurgling sound in the throat. And I whirl-snaking-turbine-shift-bucking - the white, definitive death - nobody messes with me, Mother! And the gasping of how many three four five ten cyclists who must have been passing me, or was it that I was overtaking the leaders, and for an instant I squinted over the abyss and I had to squeeze my eyelids hard and strong so all of Santiago would not take off floating and drown me, first lifting me up and then letting me fall, smashing my head against cobblestones in a street, on garbage cans full of cats, on riff-raff corners. Poisoned, with

my free hand stuck in my mouth, then biting my
wrists, I had my last moment of total clarity: an
indiscriminate certainty, untranslatable, captivating,
gradually blessed, that indeed, very well, perfect, pal,
this finish was mine, my annihilation was mine, that
all I had to do was pedal harder and win that race so
it would be played out at my death, that even I could
administer what little I had left of my body, those
throbbing toes, feverish, final, angels toes hooves
tentacles, toes claws scalpels, apocalyptic toes, definitive toes, shitty little toes, and turn the handlebars
whichever way, east or west, north or south, head or
tails, or nothing, or maybe forever stay northsouth-
eastwestheadortails, moving immobile, overwhelmed.
Then I covered my face with this hand and slapped
away the sweat and blew away my cowardice; laugh,
you imbecile, I said to myself, laugh, you wimp, laugh
because you're alone in the lead, because no one has
your fine touch with a foot in a downhill curve.

And from a final surge that came clear from the
soles of my feet, filling my thighs and buttocks and
chest and neck and forehead with beautiful, bustling,
hot blood; it was a culmination, an aggression by my
body toward God, an irresistible course, and I felt the
slope ease for a second, and opened my eyes and held
them open against the sun. Then the tires really did
smoke and squeal, the chain hummed, the handlebar
flew along like the head of a bird, sharp against the
sky, and the spokes broke the sunshine into a
thousand pieces, and scattered them everywhere.
Then I heard, my God, I heard the people cheering
me on over the pickups, the boys screaming along the
edge of the downhill curve, the loudspeaker giving the
location of the first five places. While I was coasting

on the new asphalt, one of the organizers doused me from head to foot, laughing, and twenty yards further on, dripping, laughing easily, someone looked at me, it was a red-headed girl, and she said, "soaked like a wet hen." Now it was time for me to cut the nonsense, the track was slippery, and it was once again time to be intelligent, to use the brake, to dance through the curve like I was doing a tango or waltzing to a full orchestra.

Now the wind that I was inventing (the air was calm and transparent) was stirring up the dirt into my eyes, and I almost broke my neck when I craned it around to see who was second. Blondie, of course. But only if he had a pact with the Devil would he be able to catch up and pass me on the downhill, due only to a simple reason whose technical explanation appears in sports magazines. It can be summed up like this: I never used the hand brake; I would simply jam my shoe on the tire when the curves got too sharp. Lap after lap, I was the only beast in the city bonded with his bike. The frame, the leather, the saddle, my eyes, the reflector, the handlebar, were a single form with my back, my belly, my rigid pile of bones.

I crossed the finish line and got off the bike while it was still rolling. I withstood the pounding on my back, the hugs from the coach, the photos by the guys from *Estadio*, and finished off a Coke in one big gulp. Then I took my bike and set out along the curb toward the apartment.

At the door I hesitated. It was one last moment of distrust, maybe the shadow of uncertainty, the thought that everything could have been a trap, a trick, as if the sparkle of the Milky Way, the myriad reflections of the sun in the streets, and the silence were the synopsis of a movie that would never be shown, not in the downtown theaters, not even in the cheap neighborhood movie houses, nor in the imagination of a single man.

I rang the bell, two or three times, brief, dramatic. Dad opened the door, barely a crack, as if he'd forgotten that he lived in a city where people go from house to house knocking on doors, ringing doorbells, visiting each other.

"Mama?" I asked.

The old man widened the opening, smiling.

"She's all right." He put his hand on my back and pointed to the bedroom. "Go in and see her."

I made a hell of a racket clearing my throat, and turned around in the middle of the hallway.

"What's she doing?"

"Eating lunch," Dad replied.

I went over to the bed discreetly, fascinated by the elegant way she was putting spoonfuls of soup between her lips. Her skin was livid and the wrinkles on her forehead had gotten a fraction of an inch deeper, but she was handling her spoon gracefully, rhythmically,...hungrily.

I sat on the very edge of the bed, absorbed.

"How did it go?" she asked, nibbling on a cracker.

I flashed her a Hollywood smile.

"Okay, Mama. Okay."

Her rose-colored shawl had an angel-hair noodle on the collar. I reached over to get it off. Mama stopped my hand in the act, and sweetly kissed my wrist.

"How do you feel, Mama?"

Now she ran her hand behind my neck, and then straightened the hair matted on my forehead.

"Fine, dear. Do your mother a favor, will you?"

I gestured with my eyebrows.

"Go get me a little salt. This soup is too bland."

I got up, and before going to the dining room, I went through the kitchen to see my father.

"Did you talk with her? She's revived a lot, don't you think?"

I stood looking at him while I contentedly scratched my cheek.

"Do you know what she wants, Dad? Do you know what she sent me to get?"

My old man blew out a mouthful of smoke.

"She wants salt, Dad. She wants salt. She says the soup's too bland and she wants salt."

I spun clear around on my heels and headed for the cupboard in quest of salt. When I was about to get it out, I saw the uncovered punch bowl in the middle of the table. Without using the ladle, I stuck a glass clear to the bottom, and shamelessly dribbling all over myself, poured the liquid to the bottom of my belly. It was only with the aftertaste that I could tell it was a little stale. It's my shitty old man's fault for not ever learning to put the lid on the punch bowl. I served myself another, what the hell was I supposed to do?

Fish

Wednesday morning at five o'clock as the day begins

The Beatles

When my grandmother tripped in the kitchen and the china sugar bowl shattered on the floor and the pieces scattered, my mother, who was making toast for breakfast on the gas burner, shut off the flame. She put her hands on her hips and, clamping her jaw, she hissed:

"For heaven's sake, Mama!"

The old woman puffed, but no words came out. It was like she was just getting over an asthma attack. I knew that inside Grandma's ears there were some sharp teeth gnawing deliciously on the words being said to her, and that then, as her only response, she would spit out a couple of generous squirts of saliva on the dirt patio, getting the attention of the pecking chicks.

I knew that her asthma was like an ocean that welled up in her stomach when her daughter-in-law called her "Mama." Really, they had been stalling in the last few minutes, building up a head of steam. With eyebrows raised, I bit into the rind of a day-old French roll.

While she was looking over the mess, Mom was

building up a rage. That's the way Mom was. Her motor would heat up just like that. You could never tell how hard Mom would press down on the accelerator once her motor got hot.

With her foot she pushed aside the handle of the sugar bowl, which had come off almost intact, and bent over to pick it up. "Why don't you go to your room, Mama?" she said.

I saw the old woman's glasses moving, hung around her neck on a piece of black elastic. I stuck a wad of bread in my mouth and bit off a big piece, kneading it in my mouth, with my eyes wide open.

"Go to your room, Mama! I'll bring your breakfast to you and Gramps."

Mom was picking up the pieces one by one, and Grandma's opinion was:

"It's better to sweep it up with the broom."

The trilled Yugoslavian "r" slipped out softly. She grabbed the broom from behind the door and tried to begin sweeping. Mom got up from the floor and snatched the broom away from her without looking at her.

"What could make you think about sweeping while I'm preparing breakfast?" she said. "Frankly, Mama, you're going to make my head explode."

And she put her shaking hands to each side of her head as if someone were giving her a shock treatment.

I stuck a couple of fingers in the French roll and tore off a piece. The old woman began to rock her head back and forth. She must have been about seventy; you never really know the age of a grandmother.

"You're in your own home," the old woman said.

She went to the sink, opened the tap and started

the water running.

"Mama," my mother said, "what are you doing?"

"You're in your own home," the old woman repeated.

She was picking up all the glasses in the sink as if arranging the pieces of a puzzle.

Mom looked at her and I saw the vein in her neck bulge.

"What are you doing, Madam?" she said.

"I used to have my own home," my grandmother said. "We old folks were calm and happy in my home."

She grabbed the teapot and put it under the faucet. She was stepping on the pieces of the broken sugar bowl with those fat legs of hers, covered with bandages underneath dark stockings.

"I have no age. I don't have my health," she said.

She shut off the water and carried the teapot toward the gas stove.

"Mama, go to your room," my mother said. "I'll fix your breakfast for you."

The old woman tried to pick up the match box, but she was too nervous. The match sticks scattered all over the floor. I looked through the sunlit window toward the back yard and put my hand on the latch, thinking about going to stretch out on the lawn chair.

"How long are you going to keep screwing up, Madam," my mother said.

"*How long are you going to keep screwing up,*" she repeated, separating the syllables.

I saw her give my mother a riveting glare with her blue eyes. Her wrinkled skin couldn't capture the rage she must have felt.

"This old lady isn't going to screw up anymore,"

she said, moving toward the hallway. "I'm leaving with
Pa right now." With the tip of my shoe I hid some of
the broken pieces underneath the sideboard. Mom
went out behind her, and shouted toward her room at
her:

"Do whatever you want, Ma'am!"

She went back to the kitchen. After breaking one
match, she managed to light the second one, and she
put the teapot on to heat. Dad appeared in the
doorway in his undershirt. He had just shaved, and
still had a little foam under his ears. He was carrying
his shirt in his hand, and his pale muscles distended
his short-sleeved undershirt.

"What's going on?" he asked curtly, looking at me,
but obviously asking Mom.

"What do you suppose it is?" my mother exclaimed
without looking at him. "It's Grandma again."

Dad looked at me a while longer and then busied
himself looking at the fire. He ran his hand over his
chin checking on the effectiveness of his shave. I stuck
my fingers into the bread again and pulled out a thick
wad of crumbs.

"Screw up, screw up and screw up!" Mom added,
in a confidential tone, but shouting it, really.

Dad raised his eyebrows.

"Okay," he said.

In the silence you could hear the old woman's
vague grunts. She seemed to be moving furniture. I
heard my grandfather speak. "Shit," I heard him say. I
didn't hear the rest, but I imagined it. Every time he
said "shit," he would add "Yankee, syphilitic, fantastic." At the end he would say "fucking chicken."
When the old man still had his legs, he used to go out
into the back yard to feed the laying hens, which gave

the young chicks that were loose in the patio the chance to get into the chicken coop and peck at the grain. Then he would kick them up in the air and say what I just said. He had no sympathy for the chicks. He had no sympathy for the Yankees either.

The truth is, one time he overdid it with his cleats, and he ripped open a chick, and out came the guts and everything. Grandma picked up the bird in its agony, stuffed the guts back in, and sewed it up with black thread. Then she said to Grandpa what she probably would like to forget. She said to him: "God will punish you for kicking chicks in the ass." I say that because afterwards Grandpa got gangrene and they cut off one of his legs. And later, they cut off the other one; it was two months later that they cut off the other one. And now, Gramps looks old and little in his wheelchair, and he watches every TV program there is and sometimes I take him out for a stroll along Costanera and we talk about horses.

Regarding the chick, we ate it roasted some months later. Grandma said: "This is the chicken the old man kicked."

Now Grandma entered the kitchen in grave silence. She went to the sideboard and took out two large plates of Czechoslovakian china that she had had since her wedding day. She also took out two forks and two knives. She took out spoons. Then she turned around and went to her bedroom.

"What are you doing?" Dad asked, leaning on the refrigerator.

"She says she's leaving," my mother answered, opening her arms.

"What did you say to her?"

"What do you want me to say to her. She said she's

leaving. She broke the sugar bowl."

I went into the hallway and hung around there fingering the piece of bread. Dad stuck his head through the door to the old folks' bedroom, and stood on the threshold. Grandpa, with his thick, white hair, was dishevelled, waiting for breakfast, with the empty tray resting on the sheets.

With his fingers Dad kept on checking his shave above the right corner of his mouth. I moved to his side, and we began watching all the bustle.

Grandma had opened the trunk, and was spreading out Gramps' pinstriped suit on the bed. I had seen that wardrobe opened on Sundays, when Grandma got out her rosary, her black veil and wide dress with lace. But today was Friday and she put that suit of Gramps' on the bed. It was a suit that also came out only on Sundays, but it had been two years. What I mean is that it was a suit with legs and everything. Grandpa used to dress up in that suit to go to the races. "Prince" Grandma used to call him when the old man would put on his three-piece suit and walk slowly down the main street to wait for the bus to the racetrack. That's what I remembered, leaning on the door frame next to my father. I also remembered Juan Rivera winning in a photo finish, and that we went bowling at the Arab's place and my Grandpa had this much money from Juan's horse and we bought a roasted suckling pig and a gallon jug of wine and we ate it that night at home, before Grandpa came to this house, which is my parents', and before the grocery store went to hell.

"The disease," Grandpa said, wiping off a faded green teardrop from the side of his hooked nose.

"The jackasses," Grandma said, looking over the

top of the glasses she had to use now for sewing.

Gramps, with his hands on the blanket, was swallowing saliva now and clicking his tongue, worried, looking toward the window. Grandma said something to him in Yugoslavian, and the old man made another noise with his tongue, and kept on looking at the window.

My father scratched at his ear with one finger.

"Is it okay to know what you're doing, Mama?"

The old woman kept on emptying the wardrobe. Her formal gown had appeared. I liked the way that gown smelled. It smelled like the good old days. Sometimes I would think about the great tits Grandma must have had when she was young.

"We're leaving, Son," she said, wiping the perspiration from her forehead. My granny was sweet and fat. Also pale. Fat and pale. My grandfather, on the other hand, was skinny and pale. Sunshine never touched them, and, sometimes, if I forgot about my grandfather on the patio while I amused myself reading, the fuzz on his face would curl up, and he would look at himself in the mirror and would pull out the little singed hairs.

What happens is that you can't touch old people even with the petal of a flower.

My dad had gotten quietly enthusiastic in scratching his ear with his finger.

"Where are you leaving to, Mama?"

"We're going to look for a place."

Dad nodded, and I felt him look at me sideways.

"In what boarding house, Mama?"

"I'll figure it out, Son. As long as I can work."

Dad cleared his throat without moving.

"There isn't any boarding house near here. You

would have to go downtown. In that case you're not going to be able to get on the bus with the wheelchair."

Grandma approached Gramps to take off his pyjamas. With a look of superiority, the old guy kept staring toward the picture window. Now that it was later, the sun's rays came in striking the blanket. Just by looking at it I could tell that the bed was heating up.

"Did you hear what I said, Mama?"

She was putting his shirt on him; a good shirt with a high collar and narrow blue stripes on a white background. The truth is, Grandpa had gotten skinny and the shirt was swallowing him up. He had the face of a startled bird.

"We'll go on foot, Son. As long as Granny has legs..." Dad turned his back on her and walked to the dining room. Now I realized that breakfast must be ready because the toast was giving off its aroma and Mom would be putting butter on it. Of course, Mom wasn't letting us know about anything. Today you had to guess that breakfast was ready. They had already opened the drapes, and the red checked table cloth looked pretty, with the bread basket full, the coffee steaming and the marmalade. I sat in the middle seat, opposite my mother, with my back to the hall that connected with the bedrooms. Dad scratched his hair hard and exchanged a sighing grimace with my mother. I lifted the crunchy bread to my mouth and started watching how quiet they were as they chewed. Dad dunked his French roll in his coffee with cream, let it drip in the cup, and then slurped at it, looking out the window. But looking in a very strange way, like he was spaced out. Mom also looked gone, but instead of staring out the window, she was stirring her spoon around in her coffee. What a lot of stirring, I thought, since she drinks it without sugar.

A little while passed, more or less. Meanwhile I memorized the stains on the table cloth. We took the sugar bowl and put it beside the teapot. We took the teapot and put it beside the milk, and we took off the lid of the sugar bowl. Dad whistled a march, the one from the River Kwai, and my mother was twirling her hair, with her head resting on one hand. What fascinated me was the replacement sugar bowl. It had fat blue angels on the pink china. Precisely the Sunday sugar bowl. Everything was arranged as if we were expecting company.

Suddenly a sound in the hall, the unmistakable and squeaking roll of the badly oiled wheelchair, caught my dad's attention toward the right. With my back turned, I twisted my neck, and then, leaning on the edge of the table, I turned my whole body. Dad was sipping at his cup, without looking at it, waiting for the door to open.

And, in fact, the door did open.

But Grandma didn't appear. Grandpa appeared, encased in the wheelchair rolling toward the front door. The vehicle stopped well before smashing into the door. Precisely in the middle of the room.

I now turned my whole chair around, and looked Grandpa over completely. The collar of the striped shirt had been fastened by a wide, blue tie. Smooth. And on top of that, the jacket of the three-piece suit, baggy-shouldered and slightly dusty. In regard to his trousers, you could see Grandma's practical hand. She had proceeded to fold all the excess under the chair's cushion. Which came to be more or less above the knees. But what made my eyes dart around the old man's head as if I were a bird circling its nest, was the impeccable, narrow-brimmed hat that was placed over his dishevelled forehead. I had envied him that hat on furtive incursions into the old folks' closet, beneath the nylon cover. But one time I had taken it out and had put my whole hand inside it, touching the label with my intrigued fingers. "Stetson, London," it said. Now, beneath that blackness in profile, his nose stuck out abrupt, pale. Also runny.

He only looked at us once during that long time that Grandma left the chair stuck in the middle of the room almost like a dagger stabbed into the wood, or like a spilled sack of oranges. He looked at us with green, watery eyes, but without touching us with his glance. He looked at us mutely, if you can say that. Without touching us with his glance. As if a wind had twisted his neck toward us. And immediately (I say immediately, but that's not right, it was all together, quick and without being noticed) he put one hand over the other, the two of them bony, calm and useless, and poured his gaze out into the yard.

I looked at Mom.

When she felt my stare and looked at me, I picked up the butter dish, stuck my knife into it and began to scrape a little butter onto the bread.

Dad had put on his shirt, and now he was rolling up his sleeves with almost professional care.

While I was smearing the chilled butter on the by now cold bread, I remembered my neighborhood friends. I remembered them, from when we used to trade comic books and I would leave the old guy in the shade of a kiosk until I had finished reading them. And I also remembered the day I had left a couple of comic books on the chair, and on returning, had found the old man laughing at the cartoons. Most of all I remember what they used to say to me when I would take Grandpa out for a walk. They would say: "My, what a pretty baby you've got there."

And, of course, Gramps was just a tiny piece of grandfather without his legs. With a little glance, a pretty and toothless smile. And his eyes, powerless but peaceful. Like a mirror. When the old woman appeared, she was carrying a small but wide suitcase, a basket with a skillet sticking out, a soup ladle and the large jar of Coleman brand English mustard. Also sticking out was the silver crucifix that she kept over her bed, her Bible and her rosaries. She was moving more and more heavily, and the whistling sound in her chest was getting more asthmatic. Her glasses were hanging against her chest, tied on by the black elastic.

"Take this," she said to Grandpa, handing him the suitcase. Right away she balanced it on his knees, and when she had made a solid platform, she placed the basket on it.

If I hadn't had him in profile, I would have lost Grandpa. From the front, the ladle hid his nose, and the basket handle covered his black bowler hat. The wheelchair looked like a grocery cart. I thought that Gramps, going like that, wouldn't be able to see the scenery. It's just as well, I thought right away, that the basket will shade him from the sunlight. They would have the sun to their front and up high because the cheap boarding houses were downtown. And Grandma wouldn't have much money in her black, crocheted purse.

Dad went up to Grandpa, and pushed the ladle off to the left. "How are you, Gramps?" he said to him.

He called him "Gramps," but he's the dad. Just because I exist, everyone calls Grandpa "Gramps." He used to be great at betting on the horses, and on Sunday mornings he still enjoys getting his hands on the odds. Now my dad calls his own father Gramps.

The old guy was just as still as a snapshot. As if suddenly they had painted his portrait. Dad lifted up his hat a little and with the napkin from breakfast he wiped off some black lint and a little dirt that had stuck like marks on his forehead.

"Where are you going, Gramps?" he asked.

"Syphilitic, fantastic," Grandpa said.

My mother headed for the chair at just the moment when Grandma, bathed in her wide, black dress, was appearing in the doorway and going toward Grandpa to grab the handle of the chair. Every time Grandma used to approach like that, Grandpa would lean forward a little, and he himself would lift the door latch. I would have liked to help, but it occurred to me that if I opened the door for them, it would be as if I were an accomplice to something.

So I stayed where I was, stirring the dregs of my coffee with the spoon.

Grandma had to go open the door.

In turning, she looked at us with no intent at all, almost as if she really were a visitor of ours, a visitor with a well-furnished home, a yard and a telephone, who had been invited to have breakfast and who now was returning to her luxurious routine.

In the doorway she seemed to be searching for a phrase. Perhaps something for the end of a party. One of those surprising, rhymed lines at the end of a patriotic poem. Or something from Amado Nervo. We got quieter and quieter, and we squeezed and squeezed and squeezed the silence.

The five of us seemed like a forest at night, without a breath of air, and with all the birds asleep.

I felt the squealing of the wheels leaving through the yard like a slow, serrated knife, sawing on skin, a dagger slipping into my stomach.

When the three of us were alone, I realized that Dad had put on his tie. I realized that Mom was crying, although there was no noise. My father picked up the morning edition of *El Mercurio* and started leafing through it over the remains of breakfast. Mom took a flannel rag out of her apron and started to clean up the crumbs.

As if I really didn't care one way or the other, I went out into the garden, wedging a match stick between my teeth. Our house was on a steep street, and you had to climb to get to town. So, I sat down on a streetside step and from there I watched my Grandma's wide back, which blended with the sides of the chair, climbing upward. The two of them seemed to be a single animal, an old, mangy burro, with hairs falling out like foolish signs for nobody. I thought of that story about Tom Thumb, when the asshole is scattering bread crumbs around and the fucking birds come and eat them all up. I don't know why, but as Grandma and Grandpa reached the corner, it seemed to me like they were falling apart into little pieces, which the sun caused to vibrate with a black electricity that loosened their flesh still more, like if you wiped the sweat off Grandma's forehead her face would get erased, like the black Stetson hat would eat up Grandpa. I thought I could see his green and distant eyes.

When they disappeared, I tied the laces on my

basketball shoes and started to run up the hill. In just a few yards I felt the sun stinging, as I panted. It made me itch in an unpleasant, dirty way. It didn't take me long to reach the corner. The street I was crossing was flat, full of oil stains, discreet potholes, and cracks the sun was making in the old pavement. From that moment on I stuck to the old folks from half a block away, like the dogs that follow hand carts or vegetable wagons, wagging their tails.

I saw them in the midst of the violent blinking forced on my eyes by the white sun, which poured out like glistening milk on the sidewalks. I saw them tottering in the direction of a street corner that moved ever further away. I saw them on the sticky asphalt, sliding their wheels and exhausted legs. The city was full of green, wooden houses with brown trim. They painted the houses green because there weren't any trees. The few plants along the side came up by dint of urine puddles, or of sweet old ladies with rusty peach cans who watered them. But they were plants that cast no shadow, scrawny. Some day I would make myself get out of that town. I would travel to the south and I would eat a cold melon under a broad tree. I imagined trees to be like bulls. Here I didn't see any animals; only moths that bored into the wood in the grocery stores. Rats.

But gimme a break! Rats and moths, animals? Cats, animals? I saw the old folks turn the corner and I had to run so I wouldn't lose them for an instant. Now they were going slower. They were like withering in the clear, heavy air. It was early in the morning, but, nevertheless, the sun was stinging, without giving life, withering. Just like when you put a teapot on to heat without water, and the teapot goes to shit on you.

I had an urge to let the grandparents wither alone. Let them turn into a single, old gob of black molasses abandoned on the desolate streets. I could go to the municipal pool. Swim to the raft, play with the girls from the neighborhood, pushing them under the water and submerging with them to grab them by the waist and brush against their breasts, and lie on top of them a little, on the boulders.

I saw the old folks beginning to go into a dive, like a single enormous top winding down. Just like a drunk falling against a lamp post slowly, proud, with his mouth open. I saw them squash against the sidewalk. The old woman was no longer pushing the cart, she had lain across the cart. I saw her inside the cart! What the...! I said. And I crossed the sidewalk to catch them in profile.

It was when I was holding to the walls opposite them that I saw what the old man was doing.

I saw that Grandma had, like, fainted, with all her fat across the chair, and Grandpa was pushing the wheels with both hands, as if the chair were a boat, a compact boat, and he were rowing it. And his arms were going back, and I could imagine his elbows puffing out his jacket.

Pretty old lady, I thought. Right up to the ultimate consequences, shitty old lady. She wants Grandpa, dressed like a black prince, like a dark angel, to bust a gut.

I saw the old folks, having become knotted together, twirling like a ball of twine. Maybe foaming at the mouth, how was I to know! Ah, the old folks like a black cloud, a huge, sad bird wallowing on the ground of the rigid city! Ah, the old folks, a bad cloud expelled from the galaxy in defeat so that dogs, cats and rats could piss on them!

My heart was like a pounding fist. Just like clank, clank, fuck, fuck, fuck and shit, shit, I was dragging myself back and forth, crouched down as if in a dance.

I saw Grandpa, I saw his arms like thin, powerful lances, I saw him like the worn out motor of a railroad engine, I saw him without his two legs, but with his heart holding up strong under the pounding his arms were giving it. Suddenly, reaching the shore of the dusty wall, I saw a galley ship with slaves in the hold, their veins bulging against their muscles, and above it all, like pompous birds, the English captains, young, with indifferent noses, shielding themselves with handkerchiefs against a light spray the wind was softly blowing across the deck. And below, the oarsmen, dirty, with flies on the back of their neck.

The city was the extension of a dune, and Grandpa's elbows were lagging on him. The city, a field lying fallow, like this constellation. Just like a bad dream on a Sunday afternoon, a nightmare in the sunshine at four o'clock in the afternoon. Grandpa was spinning around now in the same place. He had found a door that he couldn't get through. Immobile and deserted space had paralyzed him with the face of a squashed bird. I thought: this is his home.

I thought they're going to stay there asleep, in the white, deserted street, and the sun's rays will fall straight down on them, the sun will suck them dry like a hot sponge.

Suddenly they moved no more.

Actually, buses were passing by there, and now that I think about it, there were people in entryways, merchants with black briefcases and dazzling ties, copper-skinned working girls, young mothers with their tits exposed and their infants fussing over them. And in their midst, the old folks, like a dead tree. Just like an insignificant river that had worn out, whose last drop had been absorbed by a rotten stone, just for the hell of it.

The old folks just stayed there, painted in a bad picture, the old, asthmatic woman convulsing her shoulders, Gramps petrified on the sidewalk with his sweet-looking eyes.

I approached them with my hands in the pockets of my blue jeans, got up beside them, watching their chests expand and contract like damaged lungs; my grandma's chest, soft and wide, my grandpa's, pulsating and pale. They watched me watching them, unsurprised, almost absent. Grandma lightly raised her bent spine and riveted her chubby fingers on the bar to push the chair. Gramps took his hands away from his heart and, lifting them, crossed them over the casserole that was sticking out of the basket. Ten yards away there was a bus stop and we went there to pant in its shade. And we took our time, staying there until their bodies began to get back together. We were there about half an hour watching people go by, following them with our eyes while their shadows grew behind them. Also I was watching the buses leave, and a strange thing happened. The shadows of the buses were moving forward, and at the point of the light post, they just quickly spread out like a pool of black water. And my grandparents were also a shadow. But gray. Like the juice of something. I looked at my own shadow, too, and it was like a tree.

Suddenly Grandpa spoke.

"I'm hungry," he said.

Granny came up to him, and from above she wiped

the sweat off his damp eyebrows with a handkerchief. His forehead was dry. Grandma looked at me and easily pushed the cart.

"Let's go," she said.

At the corner I realized they were going to go clear around the block. As soon as she turned, she stopped in front of the pedlar who sold fish in baskets, chilled with ice wrapped in bags. She fished out a conger eel by the tail and rolled it back and forth in the sun watching how it reflected the light. The beast looked pretty. The pedlar weighed it in his portable scales and Grandma told him to give it to her as it was, not to skin it or cut it up.

She told the pedlar that she wanted it absolutely whole. She handed me the fish wrapped in the supplement from *El Mercurio*.

"Take it," she told me.

Now we were on the street going downhill and Granny had to hold back the little cart so it wouldn't take off. The pavement got very uneven in that stretch, and when a piece of gravel lifted the chair, Grandpa was on the verge of losing his hat. Finally he grabbed it at the level of his neck and put it back on. But he didn't put it on straight and pull it down on his forehead like Grandma had done. He put it on tilted over his left ear and kind of falling over his forehead. And then with two fingers he pretended to be holding a thick stogy, and he made like he was putting it in his mouth and supposedly was blowing smoke rings. He looked at me raising his eyebrows and said: "Humphrey Bogart."

And then he shook off the ashes like he was paddling a ping-pong ball and said: "Yankee, syphilitic, fantastic."

It was a lot easier to get the chair into the living room than to take it out. All you had to do was push down on the bar so the wheels would catch on the step. Dad had gone to work and Mom was cooking some noodles that were churning on low heat. Grandpa stayed in the dining room near the large windows, and Granny came to join me in the kitchen.

"What do you have there?" my mother asked.

Grandma unwrapped the fish and shook it purposefully by the tail.

"I bought this fish from the pedlar," she said. "I'm going to stew it, and with the skin on."

"That's the way Gramps likes it," my mother said.

I went out into the yard to read a comic book. It's true that I like to flutter around the kitchen and see what people are doing. It's true I like to watch people working. But this time I left, anxious to read comic books. I read Barbarella, an old Barrabases, and I leafed through the odds on the horses for Sunday.

I figure that quite a while must have gone by, because when Grandma called me I looked up and saw that none of the things around me cast a shadow. They were all alone and forsaken. I knew my mission. I went to the glass case and took out the napkin shaped like a bib. I went up to Gramps and hung it around his neck.

"The baby," Grandpa said.

I tied it on from behind and then I went halfway round so I could watch Grandma set down his steaming plate on the Yugoslavian tray. Gramps plunged in his spoon and blew torrentially on the first mouthful. At once he opened his mouth and tossed it in, kneading it leisurely. When he swallowed it, his lips opened wide and horizontal, and then he ran his tongue along his barren gums. Afterwards, he pulled his tongue back in and smiled.

I went out for a walk, because I can't stand fish.

Taking the Plunge

My brother takes the two straps and crosses them at the buckle on the leather suitcase he bought especially for this trip. My mom yelled at me from the kitchen to tell him to put in his galoshes in case of rain. When I told him that, he just pushed me away with an indifferent backhander.

"They'd only be a hassle," he said. "Besides, over there it's summer. Over there it doesn't rain."

I went to the kitchen, and she asked me to go back and insist on it. She doesn't believe there's any place where it doesn't rain. My mom is always hung up on getting sick; she spends all day telling you your socks are wet, that you're sweating, that you should shut the door because of the draft. Mom has a tendency to confuse the common cold with leukemia.

She's like the old bats you see in Italian movies, good for the kitchen and for spoiling kids. My dad also is like the dads in movies, and he's as good as they come, with a heart this big. Several times Pop has given away his coat in winter, and then had to buy another one on credit. A real loony is what Pop is. I have a hunch that today we're going to get the cream of the crop, because as Italian as my folks are, it's real strange that they've holed up in the kitchen and are refusing to go say goodbye to my brother. Dad said he wouldn't say goodbye to my brother for shit because last night they fought, and Mom said that Pop had told my brother he was a motherfucker. I think it's just out of solidarity that she's holed up in the kitchen, while my brother is working up a sweat trying to squeeze the other suitcase shut.

We watch him sitting on my bed smoking. I smoke all the time. That's another thing that drives my mom nuts. She says I'm going to stay little and dumb, and that I won't be like my brother, who is strong and good-looking, and buys his jackets in a swanky store on Providencia. Mama can't stand to see me with a cigarette in my snout. The other one who's smoking beside me is Paula, who's kinda like my brother's girlfriend. We're in my room and not in his because my brother doesn't like to get laid in his room: he says my room has more atmosphere. He calls atmosphere all my books and records and the posters I have stuck on the walls. My brother thinks that rooms full of books are good places to bring chicks. He has never bought books nor records because he spends his money on dressing like a fool, with Italian ties and jackets made practically on his own back. I'm just the opposite; I go around like a bum and with my hair out to here. Hair is another thing that freaks out my mom.

My brother closes the suitcases, calculates their weight, adjusts some loose straps and then puts them on the floor, apparently satisfied with the job. I think my brother is so screwed up over what my folks said about not saying goodbye to him that he's been overcome by an urge to get cultured. So he goes toward the bookshelf and looks over the books, passing a finger across them. Then he takes one out, shakes the dust from it by beating it against his thigh, raises it, and he even seems to be looking through it. He's gotta be on the verge of passing out from the intellectual effort he's making. He stops on a page, and he even appears to be reading. Although it's not very bright in here, I manage to figure out that that red book with the title in black is *Of Time and the River*, by Thomas Wolfe. Paula has raised the Venetian blinds slightly and is looking at the street. It's not that I'm checking from here, but there's no doubt it's raining. It's just that standing there, Paula has her neck twisted, looking upward as if it were raining.

"Did you read this one?"

I'm on the verge of telling him "no," so he won't take it. My brother is one of those who think that once you've read a book, you can just throw it out. He thinks that reading a book is like going to a movie. Besides, I want to be a writer, and I collect them. My mom said to me: long-hair, smoker, junkie, and now a writer: *ecco un figlio maricone*.

Finally, I don't tell him "no." I try to look him in the eye to tell him it's a good book, an outrageously good book, and that I'd give my balls for him to read it, that it doesn't matter if he takes it. But this jerk never looks anyone in the eye. He's always half-smiling and conscious of his nose. I don't know if it would be going too far or not to say that his whole face converges on his nose.

"Yes, I read it," I tell him.

"Can you lend it to me?"

"Take it."

He sits down on a chair and scans the walls and ceiling of the room. It's the tenth time in the last ten minutes I've seen him look at his watch.

"There's still time," he says.

The three of us keep silent. I hope an ant doesn't come along, because it would give us a scare. Paula changes position, moves away from the blinds, and looks around for my brother. He's staring at the wall, and I don't see where else he intends to look. I already have another cigarette butt in my hands and I light it. I go to the door. Deep down, all I want to do is get out of here. I wish this day were already over. I would have liked to cross it off the calendar. But he stops me at the doorway, calling me by the nickname I had as a little kid.

"Talk to them again," he tells me.

I come a little closer to see if when he said that, he looked at me. If he looked when he asked me to do that. I come still closer, trying to see if he is looking at me.

"Okay," I say, settling for the fact that his neck is bent over the laces of his shoes.

I go to the kitchen door, and have my pretext ready. I will go in to get a drink of water. I grab the door handle, I twist it, and *niènte*. They locked it from inside. It turns out that now you can't even get yourself a drink of water.

"Pop, let me in," I whisper through the crack, without knocking on the door.

I feel him approach.

"What do you want?"

"A glass of water, Pop."

I hear him breathe heavily. Pop must not be able to stand himself in this attitude he's assuming. I sense him in there with his ear stuck to the crack and my mom there in the background with her fingernails in her mouth.

"What glass of water, what shit, *figlio*! You're coming with messages, that's what you're coming with!"

I try the handle again.

"Open the door, Pop."

"I'm going to send him a message."

I rattle the door, still holding on to the handle.

"Tell your brother he's a traitor."

"Open the door, Dad. I want to get a drink of water." Mom must be wringing out a dish rag or scratching her cheeks. She scratches her cheeks like a fanatic every time she gets upset.

Now my dad must have lit a cigarette.

"Tell him he's a reactionary."

"Okay, Pop. Now, open the door."

"Tell him he doesn't understand a thing. That this is his home. Tell him I didn't put him through five years of college just to have him go off to who knows what son-of-a-bitch's island!"

My cigarette is just about gone. With my mouth up to the door I take the last puff.

Now he shakes the door as if he had me by the nape of the neck.

"You tell that brother of yours he's no son of mine! You just tell him that! Tell him to go away."

I could just shit for not having another smoke handy.

"Pop," I say to him, "just give him a hug and let him go. You and I are the revolutionaries, Pop. Why make a blood feud of it?"

He shakes the door again, and this time much

more energetically. I step back a little, just in case.

"There's nothing revolutionary about you! You're nothing but a jerk-off junkie! Tell your brother I didn't put him through five years..."

"Yeah, I know, Dad."

"...five years of college just so he could go off to work in who knows what shitty gas station in Australia. You tell him..." Now I pound on the door with my fists.

"Don't be a jerk, Pop!" I say to him.

I take advantage of the silence to get off my final shot. "Just shake hands with him, and that's it. If you don't do that, he'll be hurt for the rest of his life. Tell *Mom* to open the door. He asked me to tell you that. Your son wants to see you, Dad. Give him a handshake, what's it to you?"

I'm trying to hear, with my eyebrows raised, to guess with my nose what's going on. Mom, opening and closing the faucet, just for the hell of it filling glasses with water, raising them to her mouth, and then pouring them back in the sink without tasting them.

"Fuck you!" I say, and I go up the hall toward my room. I find them on my bed, kissing. In her hair, in the way it falls over her, I know that they're kissing each other differently. She, complementing the kiss with her hand on his hair, he, putting a hand under her armpit, he, searching for the edge of her ear with his tongue. I feel like these two ought to kiss each other with a whole team of translators.

I think: If he has got her pregnant, who will take responsibility? Paula was a virgin when she first came to this room. She came here with knee sox and a plaid mini skirt. Little Paula came to this room with my brother, and I went to the movies just like those jack-off kids in the jokes. I think Paula came along with my brother because of that kinda dumb thing chicks have about dudes like my brother drugging them with blah-blah. I don't see how there can still be babes who go to bed with dudes who buy their sport coats at Juven's and spend half the day smoking in front of a mirror.

Besides, she's crying. Deep in her green eyes she has a flash of light, slow-moving as if it were coming from under water. My brother must have gone over to comfort her, but then started feeling her up. When he sees me, he jumps up with a start and goes to look for a cigarette. He hands me the pack and doesn't look at me when he lights up. It's like I'm left hanging, watching Paula wipe her face with the back of her hand, then biting the back of her hand.

"What did they say?"

"They refuse to see you."

"Fucked-up old geezers."

We both take a drag on our cigarettes. With his hand, he straightens out the rippled surface of his head. He goes toward the lamp on my night stand and turns it on. It's to see what time it is.

"I need to get going."

My brother puts on his hat and whistles a tune I've also heard on the radio, but I don't remember who sings it. Then he pats his hip pocket. He checks that the dollars he has accumulated for the trip are there. He says he'll start by driving trucks, and then he'll get into a gas station.

"Go talk to the folks," he says. "Tell them I'm going."

"They refuse to see you, man. They just refuse to

see you."

He scratches his neck.

"The old man is stubborn," he says, heading toward his jacket.

I say to him: "Don't be sayin' shit like that."

He turns around, and this time he really is looking at me. He looks at me like someone who's just seen an animal come into the room. A cat, I think.

"It will be better if you go talk to the old man."

I stuff my hands in my pockets and walk toward the blinds. I open and close them. Right out front they're turning on the light. The green light on the wet sidewalk is like a sign of something. Also the red one from the stoplight. I make a knot in the cord that controls the blinds. My feet are cold, and Paula is stretched out on the bed like a blanket.

My brother kneels; he caresses her hair and kisses her on the lips. Now that I see him, he has put on his jacket. He picks up a suitcase and with a gesture he points to the other one for me. I pick it up.

"It looks like it's not raining any more," he comments. Now, with the wide suitcases getting tangled up in our legs, the hallway feels narrow to us. I walk hunched over, holding the suitcase out in front. My brother follows me with his hat on and a wave of hair falling halfway down his nose. At the front door the space widens. There is a clothes rack and a mirror. My brother steps forward and whips out his comb as swiftly as the light glints off the knife suddenly in a gangster's hand. Slowly the tuft of hair is brought to a landing. He raises an eyebrow and turns in profile, and he tilts his head still further, to see how his hair falls on his shoulder. Immediately he shakes the comb and plunges it into his handkerchief pocket. I don't know where this other cigarette between my fingers came from, with its specks of bitten-off tobacco and a red film on its end. I place the two suitcases next to the door, like we used to arrange two armies of toy soldiers symmetrically when we were kids. Suddenly it occurs to me that we're still kids. That all this is just a game. That Paula isn't really Paula, but Chabela, the maid's daughter. It occurs to me that this is just a game; that my brother will take a walk around the block, will come back with his hair all mussed up and with his cheeks scratched, and will say: I was in Africa.

Finally he puts on his white trench coat, and grabbing the lapels with the tips of his fingers, he taps them a few times to adjust them. All this, in front of the mirror. Then he turns around to talk to me. He turns his body, his tweed jacket, his Flano perfume, his James Bond trench coat, his Sinatra hat, his Italian tie, his Yamil hairdo.

But, in spite of the fact he's dressed up like a fashion plate, his voice comes out nasal and congested, like after a fight or a soccer game.

"Talk to them," he begs me.

I inhale another drag and beat on the kitchen door, which is right there, beside the front door.

"Dad," I say to him, absurdly bent over the tips of my feet and with my mouth stuck to the crack, which lets out a slim thread of light. "Dad, your son is right here. He wants to say goodbye."

Now, in the spot where I put my mouth before, I put my ear. I keep my brother's eyes in sight, while he looks upward with his neck tense, as if he wanted to hear what's going on with the nape of his neck and not with this ears.

"Dad," I repeat, urged on by a gesture of my

brother's, "put your arguments aside and talk to him. What's it to you!"

He also moves toward the crack. First we hear a murmur of voices. Mom, with a stifled cry, and him, jabbering.

My brother beats on the door, looking at it straight on, as if he were about to pass right through it. Now he has his nose up, determined, a nose that's always out front, proud like a thrusting lance, opening a path for itself. The kind of nose you see on trendy people drinking aperitifs at the Oriente or waiting for a green light in a Mercedes Benz.

I think: The old man is going to open up for him.

I think: The old man is going to vent his rage with the stab of a knife, and he's going to open this door.

Maybe all this shit is just an accident, a trick.

I think that maybe someone made a mistake in dealing out children and parents.

"Dad," my brother says.

His voice is getting softer. He whispers, finding another button to press. He doesn't want to leave wounded, he can't let anything keep on dripping within his insolent skeleton.

"Dad," my brother says, "see you later."

And he takes a step back, as if that motion were choreographed by a stage director. Between the door and him it's as if the silence were a beast. Suddenly the light from the kitchen spills over him like an embrace. I'm reminded of those pictures where the apostles appear, and straight onto their foreheads falls a ray from heaven. For a second he looks pale. For that brief second his nostrils widen and his shoulders fall, and from his waistline a brief paunch is released.

Dad appears in the vestibule, with his shirt open,

his collar doubled over, his hair gray, and his look humid and dark. Behind him Mom comes out with her kitchen rag squeezed in her hand. "Are you leaving now, *figlio*?" she says to him.

My brother nods. Then he bows his head and stares at the suitcases.

"Let me give you a hug, Pop."

Mom touches my father's back, and it's the same as if she had pushed him.

He rubs his right eyelid and stretches out his short, hairy arms. He grabs my brother and squeezes him almost as if to consume him, and then he loosens up a little, and he kisses him on the cheek, and then he squeezes him again with his eyes closed. My brother reaches his arms beneath his armpits and won't let go of his head, and he buries all the fingers of both hands in the gray hair, pressing it harder against his face.

"I hope it goes well for you, *figlio*," Dad says.

My brother won't let him go.

"Thanks," he says. And I scarcely hear him.

I think: Let him go! But instead of going toward them, I back myself against the wall.

The two detach themselves without looking at each other. Mom comes forward, takes him by the head and pulls it into the hollow of her shoulder, trapping his head between her shoulder and jaw. She sighs with her eyes closed, and her hands tremble on his head as if from infirmity.

When she lets go, my brother grabs a suitcase without looking at anyone, and for me it's like getting an order: I pick up the other one and open the door so he can leave. And we go down the stairs and we are now in the street and the lights skate across the pavement with the glint of a stabbing knife. Where did I get this cigarette I'm lighting now? Cars pass by slowly, not managing to kick up the little splash of water that has fallen since morning. My brother pats his hip pocket and walks to the curb squinting his eyes and stretching to see if he can find a taxi. With the tip of his finger he raises the edge of his sleeve and checks his watch. He inflates his mouth and then tenses it, worried.

The Chevrolet that was coming down the middle of the street closes in cautiously on the curb. We have to run a little because the car is up ahead. My brother sticks his head in the window and explains it's to the airport. First he sticks his suitcase on the front seat, and then he asks for the one I'm holding, brushing off his hands. I hand it to him and he throws it carelessly on the back seat. There's a line of cars waiting behind us. It's strange they're not honking. It's stranger still that the silence has grown with the approach of night, as if the street were full of dead birds.

My brother comes toward me and beneath the trench coat his long, quick arms are springing up and down, and he looks me in the eye seeking to envelope me with his two long arms.

But I look him in the eye and crouch.

I look him in the eye and I feel that my neck is lowered, that my teeth are glinting.

Something then holds him back.

He stays there an instant with his hands empty and ambitious, his arms full of air, like a windmill without wind, a boat without water.

Finally he lowers his arms, smiles a little, sideways, and his nose grows sharper in profile, and he raises it against the background of buildings. His smile doesn't leave him when he closes the door from inside. You can almost see the smile on the nape of his neck when the taxi pulls away showing me his back.

The kitchen door is half open, and the folks are drinking water, hushed. I filter through the hallway and get to my room. I don't know what's going on today with everything so full of silence, not even a song I could hum occurs to me. In the depths of the shadow Paula's body slowly moves. She brings her hand to her forehead to greet me, and I proceed toward the lamp and turn it off. Then I turn it on, and stand there, scraping my lower lip with my teeth. I have an urge to clear my throat, but I anticipate the noise it would make, and think better of it, slowly swallowing instead. I get a book from the shelf. I leaf through it without looking at it.

I think: When I'm big I'm going to know what to say at these moments; I'll have a snout full of words; I'll stop crouching like a cat, handling books and the shadow.

But I speak. Like a dumb little kid, my lips start moving on me.

"I have to study," my mouth says. "Tomorrow is the test." Paula says: "Excuse me."

She gets off the bed. She straightens her hair and adjusts her skirt, plunging her fingers through the belt. She takes her raincoat and picks up her purse.

I approach her, take her by the arm and stop her march toward the door.

"Don't leave," I tell her. "You have no reason to leave. I can study later. I can study not at all if I feel like it." I said it just for the hell of it. Just to say something.

"Anyway."

She is swinging her purse back and forth, and I feel

it pass over my thigh time and again.

"Don't go!"

I go toward her and arch my back to receive her. Slowly her body enters my embrace and immediately I hold her apart a little to look at her. And her eyes are sweet, and her mouth, tired, and her cheeks burn my finger tips. I kiss her on the hair, and then I kiss her on the eyes. I kiss her on the mouth. And then I hug her again. And she says nothing. And she kisses me. And from her mouth surges a moist and quick tongue, and with it she caresses my neck and then puts it in my mouth.

I take her toward the bed, and we stretch out embraced, pressing our heads together tightly, and every time we let go it's only to kiss each other. And we squeeze each other and release each other, and she says nothing, and I feel that with our tongues we're trying to reach to our throats, and I open her blouse and don't know what to say to her, and she doesn't know what to say to me, and now we only hold each other tightly.

The Composition

On his birthday, they gave Pedro a soccer ball. Pedro complained, because he wanted one made out of white leather with black patches, just like the ones the professionals use. This yellow one made of plastic seemed too light.

"You try to make a goal with a header, and it just takes off flying like a bird, it's so light."

"So much the better," his father said. "That way you won't scramble your brains."

And then he gestured with his fingers for Pedro to be quiet because he wanted to hear the radio. Over the last month, since the streets of Santiago had been filled with soldiers, Pedro had noticed that every night his dad would sit in his favorite easy chair, raise the antenna of the green appliance, and listen intently to news that came from far away.

Pedro asked his mother: "Why do you always listen to the radio with all that static?"

"Because what it says is interesting."

"What's it say?"

"Things about us, about our country."

"What things?"

"Things that are going on."

"And why is it so hard to hear?"

"Because the voice is coming from far away."

And Pedro sleepily looked out over the mountain range framed by his window, trying to figure out over which peak the radio voice was filtering.

In October, Pedro starred in some great neighborhood soccer games. He played in a tree-lined street, and running through the shadows in spring was almost as pleasant as swimming in the river during the summer. Pedro imagined that the rustling leaves were the sound of an enormous grandstand in some roofed stadium, applauding him when he received a precision pass from Daniel, the grocer's son, and made his way, like Simonsen, through the big kids on defense, to score a goal.

"Goal!" Pedro would shout, and he would run to hug everyone on his team, and they would pick him up and carry him like a kite or a flag. Though Pedro was already nine years old, he was the smallest kid for blocks around, so they nicknamed him "Shorty."

"Why are you so small?" they would ask him sometimes, to pester him.

"Because my dad is small and my mom is small."

"And for sure your grandpa and grandma too, because you're itty-bitty, teeny-tiny."

"I'm small, but I'm smart and quick. When I get the ball, nobody can stop me. The only quick thing you guys have is your tongue."

One day Pedro tried a quick move along the left flank, where the corner flag would be if that had been a perfect soccer field, and not a dirt street in the neighborhood. When he got to Daniel, the store owner's son, he faked a move forward with his hips, stopped the ball so it rested on his foot, lifted it over Daniel's body, who was face down in the dirt already, and made it roll softly between the stones that marked the goal.

"Goal!" Pedro shouted, and ran toward the center of the playing field, expecting a hug from his team mates. But this time no one moved. They were standing motionless, looking toward the store. A few windows opened and eyes appeared, staring at the corner as if some famous magician or the Circus of Human Eagles with its dancing elephants had just arrived. Other doors, however, had been slammed shut by an unexpected gust of wind. Then Pedro saw that Daniel's father was being dragged away by two men, while a squad of soldiers was aiming machine guns at him. When Daniel tried to approach, one of the men stopped him by putting a hand on his chest.

"Take it easy," the man yelled at him.

The store owner looked at his son.

"Take good care of the store for me."

The jeep took off, and all the mothers ran outside, grabbed their kids and took them back inside. Pedro stood by Daniel in the middle of the dust cloud raised by the departing jeep.

"Why did they take him away?" he asked.

Daniel stuck his hands in his pockets, and at the bottom he squeezed the keys.

"My dad is a leftist," he said.

"What's that mean?"

"That he's antifascist."

Pedro had heard that word before, the nights his dad spent next to the green radio, but he didn't know what it meant, and most of all, it was hard for him to pronounce. The "f" and the "s" rolled around on his tongue, and when he said it, a sound full of air and saliva came out.

"What does anti-fa-fascist mean?" he asked.

His friend looked at the long, empty street and told him, as if in secret:

"That they want our country to be free. For Pinochet to leave Chile."

"And for that they get arrested?"

"I think so."

"What are you going to do?"

"I don't know."

A worker came slowly toward Daniel and ran a hand through his hair, leaving it more mussed than ever.

"I'll help you close up," he said.

Pedro headed home kicking the ball, and since there was no one in the street to play with, he ran toward the next corner to wait for the bus that would bring his father home from work. When he arrived, Pedro hugged him around the waist and his father bent over to give him a kiss:

"Hasn't your mother come home yet?"

"No," the boy said.

"Did you play a lot of soccer?"

"A little."

He felt his father's hand take his head and hug it against his jacket.

"Some soldiers came and took Daniel's dad prisoner."

"Yes, I know," his father said.

"How did you know that?"

"They called me."

"Daniel is in charge of the store now. Maybe now he'll give me candy."

"I don't think so."

"They took him away in a jeep. Like the ones you

see in the movies."

His father said nothing. He breathed deeply and stood looking sadly down the street for a long time. In spite its being daylight and springtime, only men returning slowly from work were out in the street.

"Do you think it will be on TV?"

"What?" his father asked.

"Don Daniel."

"No."

That night the three of them sat down to dinner, and although no one told him to be quiet, Pedro didn't say a word, as if infected by the silence with which his parents were eating, looking at the designs on the table cloth as if the embroidered flowers were in some far-off place. Suddenly his mother started to cry, without making a sound.

"Why's Mom crying?"

His dad first looked at Pedro, and then at her, and didn't answer. His mother said:

"I'm not crying."

"Did someone do something to you?" Pedro asked.

"No," she said.

They finished dinner in silence, and Pedro went to put on his pyjamas, which were orange, with a lot of drawings of birds and rabbits. When he came back, his mother and father were sitting on the sofa with their arms around each other, and with their ears very close to the radio, which was giving off strange sounds, made more confusing than ever by the low volume. As if guessing that his father would put his finger to his mouth and gesture for him to be quiet, Pedro quickly asked:

"Dad, are you a leftist?"

The man looked at his son, and then at his wife,

and immediately both looked at him. Then he nodded his head slowly up and down, in assent.

"Are they going to take you prisoner, too?"

"No," his father said.

"How do you know?"

"You bring me good luck, Kid," the man said smiling.

Pedro leaned on the doorjamb, pleased that they weren't sending him directly to bed, like other times. He paid attention to the radio, trying to figure out what it was that drew his parents to it every night. When the voice on the radio said "the fascist junta," Pedro felt that all the things that were rolling around in his head came together, just like when one at a time the pieces of a jigsaw puzzle fit together into the figure of a sailing ship.

"Dad!" he exclaimed then. "Am I antifascist, too?"

His father looked at his wife as if the answer to that question were written in her eyes, and his mother scratched her cheek with an amused look until she said:

"You just can't tell."

"Why not?"

"Children aren't anti-anything. Children are simply children. Children your age have to go to school, study a lot, play hard, and be kind to their parents."

The next day, Pedro ate a couple of French rolls with jelly, got one finger wet in the sink, wiped the sleep out of his eyes, and took off on the fly to school so they wouldn't mark him tardy again. On the way, he found a kite tangled in the branches of a tree, but no matter how much he jumped and jumped, there was no way.

The bell hadn't stopped ringing when the teacher

walked in very stiff, accompanied by a man in a military uniform, with a medal as long as a carrot on his chest, a gray moustache, and sun glasses blacker than the dirt on your knee. He didn't take them off, maybe because the sun was coming in the room like it was trying to set it on fire.

The teacher said:

"Stand up, children, and very straight."

The children got up and waited to hear from the officer, who was smiling with his toothbrush moustache below his dark glasses.

"Good morning, my little friends," he said. "I am Captain Romo, and I have come on behalf of the government, that is to say, on behalf of General Pinochet, to invite all the children from all the classes in this school to write a composition. The one who writes the nicest composition of all will receive personally from General Pinochet a gold medal and a ribbon like this one with the colors of the Chilean flag."

He put his hands behind his back, jumped to spread his legs, and stretched his neck out, raising his chin slightly.

"Attention! Be seated!"

The children obeyed, scratching themselves as if they didn't have enough hands.

"All right," the officer said, "take out your notebooks.... Notebooks ready? Good! Take out a pencil.... Pencils ready? Write this down! Title of the composition: 'My home and my family.' Understood? In other words, what you and your parents do from the time you get home from school and work. The friends who come over. What you talk about. Comments when watching TV. Whatever occurs to you with complete freedom. Ready? One, two, three: let's begin!"

"Can we erase, sir?" one boy asked.

"Yes," said the captain.

"Can we write with a Bic pen?"

"Yes, young man, of course!"

"Can we do it on graph paper, sir?"

"Certainly."

"How much are we supposed to write, sir?"

"Two or three pages."

The children raised a chorus of complaint.

"All right, then, one or two. Let's get to work!"

The children stuck their pencils between their teeth and began looking at the ceiling to see if inspiration would descend on them through some hole. Pedro was sucking and sucking on his pencil, but he couldn't get a single word out of it. He picked his nose and stuck a booger that happened to come out on the underside of his desk. Leiva, his deskmate, was chewing off his fingernails one by one.

"Do you eat them?" Pedro asked him.

"What?" his friend said.

"Your fingernails."

"No. I bite them off with my teeth, and then I spit them out. Like this. See?"

The captain approached down the aisle, and Pedro could see his hard, gilded belt buckle from just inches away.

"And aren't you working?"

"Yes, sir," Leiva said, and as fast as he could, he furrowed his brow, stuck his tongue between his teeth and put down a big "A" to start his composition. When the captain went toward the blackboard to talk with the teacher, Pedro peeked at Leiva's paper.

"What are you going to put down?"

"Whatever. And you?"

"I don't know."

"What did your folks do yesterday?"

"The same old thing. They came home, ate, listened to the radio and went to bed."

"That's just what my mom did."

"My mom started to cry all of a sudden."

"Women go around crying all the time, didn't you ever notice?"

"I try not to cry ever. I haven't cried for over a year."

"And if I beat the shit out of you?"

"What for, if I'm your friend?"

"That's true."

The two stuck their pencils in their mouths and stared and stared up at an unlit bulb and the shadows on the walls, and their heads felt as empty as their piggy banks and as dark as a blackboard. Pedro put his mouth close to Leiva's ear and said:

"Listen, Skinny, are you antifascist?"

Leiva kept an eye on the captain. He gestured for Pedro to turn his head, and said, breathing into his ear:

"Of course, you dumb shit!"

Pedro scooted away a little bit and winked at him, just like the cowboys in the movies. Then he leaned toward his friend again, pretending to write on the blank paper:

"But you're just a kid!"

"That doesn't matter!"

"My mom told me that kids..."

"That's what they always say.... They arrested my dad and took him north."

"They did that to Don Daniel, too."

"I don't know him."

"The store owner."

Pedro looked at the blank page, and read his own handwriting:

"What My Family Does at Night," by Pedro Malbran, Syria School, Third Grade-A.

"Skinny," he said to Leiva, "I'm going to try for the medal."

"Go for it, man!"

"If I win, I'll sell it and buy a professional-size, white, leather soccer ball, with black patches."

"That's if you win."

Pedro wet the end of his pencil with a little spit, sighed deeply, and started writing without interruption.

A week went by, during which one of the trees in the neighborhood fell over just from old age, a kid's bike was stolen, the garbage man didn't come by for five days, and flies blundered into people's faces, and even got into their noses, Gustavo Martínez, from across the street, got married, and they gave big pieces of cake to the neighbors. The jeep came back and carried off Professor Manuel Pedraza under arrest, the priest refused to say Mass on Sunday, Colo Colo won an international match by a huge score, and the school's white wall had a red word spread across it: "Resistance." Daniel got back to playing soccer and made one goal *de chileno* and another *de palomita*, the price of ice cream cones went up, and, on her eighth birthday, Matilde Schepp asked Pedro to kiss her on the mouth.

"You must be nuts!" he responded.

After that week, still another went by, and one day

the captain came back with an armful of papers, a bag of candy and a calendar with the picture of a general.

"My dear little friends," he said to the class, "your compositions are very nice and the armed forces have been very pleased with them. On behalf of my colleagues and of General Pinochet I must congratulate you very sincerely. The gold medal didn't come to this class, but to another, somebody else got it. But to reward your nice work, I'm going to give each one of you a piece of candy, your composition with a note on it, and this calendar with a picture of our illustrious leader on it."

Pedro ate his candy on the bus, on the way home. He stood on the corner waiting for his father to get home, and later, he put his composition on the dining room table. At the bottom, the captain had written in green ink: "Bravo! Congratulations!" Stirring at his soup with a spoon in one hand, and scratching his belly with the other, Pedro waited for his father to finish reading it. His father handed the composition to his wife, and looked at her without saying anything. He started on his plate and didn't stop until he had eaten the last noodle, but without taking his eyes off her.

The woman read:

When my dad gits home from work, I go wait for him at the bus stop. Sometimes my mom is in the house and when my dad comes in, she says to him hi, how'd it go today? Okay, my dad says, and how did it go for you? Okay, my mom says back. Then I go out and play soccer, and I like to try to make goals with headers. Daniel likes to play goalie and I get him all worked up because he can't intercept me when I spike

*one at him. Then my mom comes and says it's time to
eat, Pedro, and we sit down to eat, and I always eat
everything except the beans, which I can't stand.
Afterwards, my dad and mom sit on the sofa in the
living room and play chess, and I do my homework.
And after that we all go to bed, and I try to tickle
their feet. And after that, way after that, I can't tell
any more because I fall asleep.*

Signed: Pedro Malbran

*P.S. If you give me a prize for my composition, I
hope it's a soccer ball, but not a plastic one.*

"Well," his dad said, "we'll have to buy a chess set,
just in case."

The Cigarette

You ain't nothin', man,
neither fish nor fowl,
you're too busy stroking -
caramba zamba - your own dignity.

Victor Jara

She saw the boy as he jumped on the other one who
was down, and she liked the way the light shown
almost horizontally along the part in his hair. With a
premonition she rushed to join the other women who
blocked the scene by forming a circle.

The one on the ground, with his legs raised, was
kicking furiously.

If you came at him from behind he would be
defenseless.

The boy with the helmet looked at her a second,
and, as if following the orders in her mind, circled
around, swinging the chain. When he got across from
her, she said to him:

"Kill him."

He blinked and the sun reddened his bony nose
beneath the helmet, and the chain hummed through
the air, fell like the clapper of a bell, like the crack of
a whip, and slashed open the temple of the fallen boy.

The woman crossed toward him and squeezed
his arm.

One of the men made his way through the group

and went toward the boy.

"The cops are coming."

The young man cast a last glance at the body on the asphalt and straightened his trousers, pulling them up by the belt.

"Let's go," the woman said to him.

By now women were banging ladles on pots along the entire avenue. The armed young men who were parading along the flanks craned their necks looking for any supporters of the People's Government to appear.

The boy had draped his sweater over his shoulders, and secured it by crossing the sleeves in a knot on his chest. As they went on, he wiped his forehead with his sleeve and breathed deeply.

"I really fixed that guy," he said.

"Hurry up."

"I knocked his block off, did you see?"

"We'd better hurry. They took pictures."

For the first time the young man seemed to notice the woman's pressure on his arm. He looked at her down to her plunging neckline, and again went over her fine, mature face, the small teeth, the elegant wrinkles covered with a layer of opaque powder.

"They took pictures?" he asked, raising a hand to his helmet.

"Let's hurry up," the woman said.

They crossed the avenue, and before entering the modern building, he glanced back toward the shreds of the parade that was beginning to dissolve in Plaza Italia.

"There aren't many of the old women, but they squawk so nice it's a pleasure to hear them," the young man said.

He looked at the woman and saw that she was scrutinizing him, too. At that moment the boy thought she also was one of those old women, that he had included her among those old bags. But instantly the woman's mouth opened into a pretty smile.

In the elevator, she said to him: "And what if you killed that guy?"

The young man froze, surprised: "He was moving, wasn't he?"

"Agreed, but sometimes those blows affect the brain. Suppose they take him to the hospital and he dies."

He felt that the woman was only trying to scare him a little with her serious look. "No one dies from a blow like that one," he thought.

He saw that the woman was smiling now. And then he saw the green Otis "stop" button. He felt an irresistible impulse to get out of the elevator and go back to the spot where the man was. "Without the helmet," he immediately corrected himself. When the door opened, the woman softly and bubblingly parodied a servant who yields the way to her master, and the young man mimicked the pompous master who bestows a gratuity. She was first to cross the stretch to the apartment, jingling her keys loudly. Inside, she walked straight down the hall, and went directly to the liquor cabinet. From a large bottle of Scotch she half-filled two glasses.

"I'll get some ice," she said.

The young man yanked off his helmet and, putting his hand inside, twirled it around on one finger. He kept up this motion until the woman returned with the ice cubes.

"I didn't think you had such long hair," she said.

"Like this, without the helmet, you look great."

He took the chain out of his pocket and placed it on the table, right next to the glasses. Then he noticed the portion of steel that had blood stains. The woman noticed it at the same time, and she also noticed in his eyes, or, more still, on his lips, the burden of fear.

"You did what you had to do," she told him.

"Sure."

They lifted their glasses to their mouths, and he rubbed his chin with his hand when he had finished.

"That's a great Scotch," he commented.

"Cheers," the woman said, refilling his glass.

She waited until the young man had finished his second dose to help herself to the liquid in her own glass. Then she refilled both glasses.

They walked toward a sofa, and she turned on a floor lamp adorned with a filigree of Persian motifs. The young man discarded his sweater, and with quick dancing movements in his fingertips, he undid the ample row of buttons on his shirt. "Excuse me," he said to the woman, showing her his exposed chest, "it's the heat."

She held out a handkerchief and rubbed it over his hairless chest. Atop his body, rather suddenly, she slid her lips over the boy's skin, and sticking her tongue out she slowly licked his nipples. The young man let her do that to him for a moment, but then he shoved her away, plunging a hand into her hair.

"I don't like you to do that to me," he said.

The woman managed to blink, and during that fraction of a second she changed her look into an aristocratic, superior, icy expression. When the boy had said that to her, he was looking her in the eye, and now it was as if he realized that he had been insolent. Although he didn't know the woman, she was just like the congressman's wife who gave them instructions and arms. He felt that once again he was in front of his boss, and it was hard to swallow.

"Excuse me," he said, looking at the liquid in the glass. "It's just that when you kiss me there it makes me feel.... I don't know. That's for queers..."

The woman squeezed her cheeks into a disparaging smile. "Maybe you are a queer," she said to him, feigning softness, almost tenderness.

"No," he replied, "it's just that there are some things I don't like."

She rested her neck on the back of the sofa and began playing around with her feet.

"And fame, do you like that?"

He turned to look at her but she didn't take her eyes off the ceiling.

"What?"

"Fame. To be famous. Wouldn't you like to be famous?"

"I guess so. Why wouldn't I want to be famous?"

She leaned forward, and, stretching out her fleshy mouth, ran it over the young man's nose and planted an indifferent kiss on it.

"Tomorrow a picture of you beating up a poor communist will come out in the papers. All of Chile will want to know who that strange little young man is, so luscious, so handsome, with such gorgeous hair, who is beating the shit out of some poor kid."

The young man went to the table and served himself another dose of whiskey.

"Why do you say that, lady? Why are they going to publish my picture beating the shit out of some commie?"

She lifted a finger and flicked the end of his nose. Then she lowered the same finger to her own mouth, squeezing it into a pout, and caused it to make the sound "sh."

"Cheers," the boy said. "It's idiocy. They won't recognize me with the helmet."

The woman went to the table and capped the whiskey bottle. At once she ran her fingernails over the boy's skin until they reached his waistline. She passed her moist lips, still carrying the aroma of whiskey, over his neck and offered him her perfumed hair to smell. He abruptly grabbed her by the buttocks and pressed her abdomen against his. She drove her fingers into his hair and twisted her head to kiss him on the mouth. He pushed her away and rubbed his eyelids hard with the back of his hands. "Excuse me," he said. "I'm nervous."

"Because of the picture?"

She still had a hand hooked into his belt.

"You have nothing to worry about."

He chewed on his fingernails.

"Let me get another drink."

"I'll get it for you."

She filled the new glass, violently dropping in an ice cube. "I have to go," the young man said then, picking up his sweater from the table.

"Where to?"

"I have to see what happened. I have to see if I killed him."

The woman thrust the glass into his hand.

"Don't be a jerk. You haven't killed anyone."

"You told me to kill him."

"Nobody dies from one blow with a chain, does he?"

"I have to see."

"Where?"

The young man blinked, surprised. He tied the sweater on with a knot over his chest again, just as he had seen the kids do walking along Providencia Avenue.

"I don't know," he said. "I'll ask someone."

"Who? How? 'You, sir, have you seen a guy I hit lying on the ground dead?'"

Anticipating his movement toward the helmet, she intercepted him and put it on his forehead, crooked. He tried to laugh, but the result was an unenthusiastic grimace.

"This helmet is your salvation. No one will be able to recognize you."

"It's not a problem if they recognize me. I think maybe that boy is dead."

She froze the look on her face while he sipped at his whiskey.

"And then?"

"What?"

"You killed a communist, that's all."

The young man raised his fingers to his mouth and devoutly nibbled a thumbnail.

"That's also true," he said. "But to kill anyone..." The woman lit a cigarette and, after drawing on it, offered him a drag.

"Lady, I'm nervous."

The woman went toward the door.

"Goodbye, hero," she said to him.

The young man walked bumping along the walls of the hallway. On the threshold he turned toward her.

"Thanks, lady," he said.

The woman fit the helmet on his head and draped

the chain on his arm.

"Take your arsenal with you, hero."

Outside the apartment, he felt his apprehension growing. A kind of weepiness almost, but just almost, built up on the sides of his nose. He thought it was idiotic to go out on the street with the helmet and chain. Then he went to the incinerator, and, opening the small door, threw them in without thinking any more about it.

In the elevator, with his eyes closed, he tried to reconstruct the scene. There was a moment, a special moment when, in the midst of the uproar, he had stopped, raised his face, and the woman had spoken to him. Had she said "kill him"?

In the street the march had dissolved, and the sound of pots could be heard only on the Providencia side. He thought about walking in that direction and going to the congressman's house to meet up with the other paramilitary groups, but he gave up that idea, without stopping to consider it further.

He got on a bus that was going down Alameda Avenue, and the wind coming through the window produced a refreshing, calm sensation. He leaned his head on the back of the seat, and at that moment he felt certain that the boy had not died. "He didn't die," he said, nodding his head in the negative.

At the bus stop he got off and started to trot, and then to run, toward his mother's house. The dirt footpath along the streets of the subdivision was uneven and full of stones, and after his first stumble he kept on jumping along, attentive to the unevenness of the road. Once he surprised himself looking back, attempting to scrutinize the dark streets for anyone who might be following him.

Through the window, he saw his mother setting the table, smoothing out with her palms the same checkered table cloth from his childhood. He knocked on the window, the woman approached to identify him, and immediately smiling, went to open the door. "Are you alone, Mom?"

Now he noticed that there, inside, he was also looking for someone else in the room.

"Yes," his mother said. "Your sister had to work a shift at the bar and grill, and afterwards, a party meeting."

She noticed that the boy was panting.

"What's wrong with you?"

"I came here running."

"Is something wrong?"

"No, Mom. I just ran here."

His mother handed him a glass of water. The young man drank it in two gulps, and as he was leaving the glass on the table, he almost knocked it over. He managed to grab it in a brusque motion, and noticed that the woman was looking at him alertly.

"There was a brawl downtown," he said.

He went to the easy chair and plopped down crossing his feet.

"I heard about the march," she said.

"What did they say?"

"They said there was a brawl. What's wrong with you?"

She drew up a chair, sat down next to the young man and leaned over him. The boy averted his glance and ran it over the familiar stains on the wall.

"Nothing, Mom," he said, feigning a smile.

The woman took out a pair of glasses and put them on, fitting the frame energetically to her ears.

"I was in a fight," the boy said. "I was working with those in the march and I fought with some lower-class trash who insulted us."

He put his feet together and began to stomp on the floor. His mother leaned her whole body against the back of the chair and rubbed her forehead without looking away from him.

"Some *lower-class trash*?"

"Please, Mom."

"Just a minute, Son. You say you hit some *lower-class trash*?"

The boy saw that his mother's face was stern, but holding back tears, moist, on the verge.

"Well, yeah, Ma, but don't get things all mixed up. For a long time I haven't..."

"And what are we, then?"

The boy patted his pockets.

"It's not the same, Ma. You're my mom."

Now the woman was breathing in short, strenuous puffs. "*You* were in that march fighting for them? Who do you think you are, by the Holy Virgin? By God in heaven, who the devil do you think you are?"

The young man jumped up to get a pack of cigarettes from the shelf.

"Please, Ma. You don't understand about these things. Gotta match?"

The woman grabbed him tight by the arm. The cheeks on her face had compressed into a grimace of astonishment.

The young man patted his pockets.

"I have my ideas, Mom. Give me some matches, will you?"

He looked at the woman's hand on his arm and then he scratched his head.

"Everyone to his own thing, Ma. Don't you get it?"

He looked toward different parts of the room and went back to patting his pockets.

"Do you have any matches, Mom?"

"What did you come here for?" she asked him, intensifying the pressure on his arm.

"Let me go, Ma."

He thrust his hands into his pockets and walked toward the window.

"I wanted to spend the night here, understand?"

"What did you do to him?"

"Nothing, Mom. We had a fight, what was I supposed to do?" For a minute they stood silent without looking at each other. The boy rubbed his eyelids hard and picked up the sweater from the easy chair.

"I'd better leave," he said.

He crossed the sleeves of the sweater tying it over his chest. The woman went to the table and flattened out a wrinkle in the table cloth.

"Stay if you want," the woman said.

"I'm leaving," the boy said.

In the street he switched the unlit cigarette to the other side of his mouth, pushing it with his tongue. All the way to the corner he was certain his mother would come out into the street and call to him, asking him to come back. But going through the first intersection, when the dog crossed his path, he thought that she wouldn't be able to handle this much of a delay.

He was the first to get on the bus. For an instant he wavered in the aisle among all the vacant seats. It crossed his mind that it was idiotic to think about it, but he would have preferred if there had only been one vacant seat in the bus, so he wouldn't have to choose. Finally, he situated himself on the long seat of the back row. From there, at the next block, he saw a big group of young factory workers get on, almost all with long hair wetted down by gel, which gave their heads a hard and glossy look. From their arms hung blue canvas bags, just like the ones the boy himself had used for gym class at school. They moved through the bus slapping each other and exchanging gibes with thin smiles full of teeth, and like all such groups, they crowded together in the last seats.

The young man thought that they must be coming from a soccer game, and, distracted, he didn't change his position on the seat, so he ended up between two groups of laborers. In three minutes the bus was full of laughter, and short necks were hunching down quickly to avoid the slaps intended to violate their impeccable coiffures. Each time that happened, the laborers took out plastic combs and smoothed out their manes, lifting their waves with the back of their hands.

Suddenly, a grazing slap fell on the young man's ear, while at the same time they exerted such a pressure from his left side that he slid out of the seat, falling to the floor. Simultaneously, from the left end of the group he heard the voice of the youngest of the boys shout: "Look, the filling just dropped out of our sandwich!"

And immediately: "Cut it out, guys."

Two arms, one on each side, picked him up and put him back in his place on the seat. He hardly had time to feel humiliated. He scarcely managed to look at the swarthy guy with a moustache on his right: "Pardon us," the latter said to him. "The boys always get to playing around like this."

And the blond guy on the other side: "You dropped your cigarette."

He had the unlit cigarette in his hands, and he was holding it near the boy's mouth. The boy stretched out his lips, and biting on the filter a little, made a gesture of gratitude. "It's okay," he said.

"Cut the shit, boys," shouted the guy with the moustache.

"It's okay," the young man said. Suddenly he added: "My dad worked in the same factory as you do."

"What's his name?" asked the one with the blond hair.

Now he realized that they were all looking at him.

"No. He died," the young man said.

The boys continued looking at him, interested.

"He died a long time ago," he said. "You must not have gotten to know him."

The guy with the moustache nodded in agreement. The laborers in the front seats turned their faces and started to look out the window. There was a silence, and you could hear only the rattling or the squealing brakes of the Pegaso bus. After a while, the young man turned toward the guy with the moustache and said: "My old man was one of the directors of the union."

The other one nodded gravely, although smiling slightly. "It's a pity your father died," he said. "He would have liked to be alive now, because the factory is ours. We're in socialist territory now, comrade."

"Of course," said the blond on the other side.

"Okay," the boy said.

He got off in Italia Plaza, and as soon as he hit the ground he patted his trouser pockets looking for matches. Then he noticed that the cigarette filter was too chewed up. He felt the inner fibers on his lips, and taking it out of his mouth, he moved it to between the fingers of his right hand.

In the elevator there was a mirror. After glancing askance, to check that his hair looked elegant, he again inserted the cigarette between his teeth.

When the woman opened the door, he told her: "It's all okay. There was no death."

"I told you so," the woman assured him.

She went to the coffee table in the living room and picked up a fine, footed lighter with inlaid mother-of-pearl. The flame was tenuous but efficient at the press of her thumb. He looked at the woman and lit the cigarette, inhaling deeply. He expelled the smoke with his mouth wide open and said: "I was at my mother's place."

She crossed her arms and looked at him with an indifferent expression. The boy approached her taking a new drag, and added: "She couldn't give me a light."

The young man took the cigarette from his lips and an absent look crossed his face. But at the same time, the woman came forward to unfasten the top button of his shirt. The boy smiled, and while he embraced her he looked sidelong toward the table.

"I'd like a little more of that booze," he said.

Man with a Carnation in His Mouth

"I feel anguish, longing,
But not with all my being. Something
Deep within me, something deep in there -
Cold, heavy, mute - remains."

Fernando Pessoa

The girl skirted the trees with the quick impulse of a woman alone in a public place, somewhere between dignified, cautious and distracted, as if her solitude were shameful and as though the mouths of all men were about to kiss her on the neck or nibble at her lips.

She assumed the look of someone with a particular destination until she got all the way across the plaza. When she reached the other side, she stopped, giving herself time to take a deep breath. Her shoulders relaxed, her chin was forced downward by a smile, and she made a gesture of self-encouragement with her elbows. Once again she had caught herself acting like the obedient child of the very tensions and formalities she despised: the distrust, the misery of holding false expressions on her face, the egotism of useless proprieties. She thought: "Just like I used to walk home from high school. Just like I used to walk to the movies every Sunday. We all walked alike. As if our solitude made us into whores."

The men and women in the plaza lifted their wrists to check the time. They compared their watches, glanced up the side streets, and looked toward the sky as if hoping that all their restlessness would fasten on to something. They were together, but in the same way that the survivors of a very lively party stay together; clumsily fingering the arm of the record player when there is no longer any music that can possibly satisfy everyone. There were only seconds left, and no one wanted the old year to go out the way you just toss a letter in the mailbox.

They looked toward the corners again. They also kept looking insistently at the sky, putting their wrists to their ears, and the girl felt the flower above her ear flutter in the breeze. Then she realized there was a man standing behind her.

And at the exact moment the hugging began, she also realized it was that man who was hugging her, although not with a frontal, strident, emphatic New Year's embrace. Rather, it was with a half-embrace, the insinuation of an embrace, the way one leans on a familiar shoulder, but also with the softness of someone who knows that the shoulder is fragile.

She wanted to stay within that unknowing, amusing silence, caught in that anonymous grasp, surrendering herself to the rest of the scene, the characters, the unreal lighting decor, the city, Portugal, and the universe. But she had already turned her head and, with a slight tension in her eyes, was looking curiously at the boy's features. In return, he gave her only a distracted, relaxed, accidental smile, the way he would if he had been hanging on her shoulder for three nights – as if, bored by now from chatting with her, he were concentrating on the small eccentricities of the passers-by, their shouts and greetings – just as if he were an expert at shouts and greetings.

Using great dexterity, the young man took the carnation he had been holding in his mouth by the stem with his tongue, and in an odd pirouette, moved it to the left corner of his mouth. He kept it there with his jaws clamped shut.*

That was the moment when the girl revised the "Happy New Year" she had in mind, and decided just to let her body's fluency speak for her.

"If it matters, that's my shoulder," she said.

"Yes, I know," blurted the young man (younger than she), without looking at her (but managing to look at her, all the same). "I leaned on yours because my own no longer interests me."

In order to talk with her he held the stem of the carnation with his teeth. She lifted her free hand and poked at the flower with her finger.

"It looks like you're a vegetarian, right?"

"No, I never eat them. I just hold them in my mouth."

The crowd in the plaza began to surge feverishly toward the corner on the left. From a side street, preceded by horn honking and the chant of "A people once united can never be divided," a chaotic line of students and workers came forward. Both of them let themselves be carried along by the wave, going down the street until they joined the head of the march. An old man with a sharp nose, thick glasses, and a noticeable limp, was holding up the pole of a huge red flag. Even though people enthusiastically applauded as he passed by, the man seemed absent, surrounded by a small aura of glory, attentive to a symphony performed in his head for him alone.

*Translators' note: The carnation was a symbol of opposition to the fascists in Portugal.

They marched a little in front of him, without letting go of each other, while in the plaza circles formed to the rhythm of the same chant. Spewing bottles appeared everywhere. They appeared from car windows, and flag-waving cyclists were bringing them in. The isolated pop of champagne corks sounded amid the shouting, chanting and honking, jumbled by a breeze that was barely cool, just as if it were not winter.

The young man led her apart to the Piquenique Restaurant and gestured for her to sit down at the snack bar. They ordered two sandwiches and a good red wine.

"Well," he said, "my name is Jorge."

"Carmen," the girl said.

They shook hands and waited for the wine in silence. Meanwhile they looked at each other a little, with amused smiles and vague gestures. She concluded that it wasn't in the young man's style to ask anything further, although it was in hers. But, finally, she didn't ask anything either. The wine came, and they drank the first glass with conspiratorial haste. The girl savored its taste and its warmth against her cheeks. He collapsed on the counter laughing and buried his face in his arms, shaking for a few seconds while she served up another round. Then he raised his face, wiped off his moist cheeks, and put the carnation in the gap between his front teeth. Nodding to himself, he forced himself not to laugh any more.

"I'm very happy," he said in Spanish.

"I can see that," the girl said.

"I was in prison a year. My old man was in prison five years, until he escaped. He died in France."

With her eyebrows the girl invited him to raise his

glass of wine. The steaming sandwiches were put on the counter, and they ate them avidly. When there was nothing but a few crumbs left, and the waiter had finished off the bottle, pouring it in their glasses with professional dexterity, the boy said: "Now, I'll pay up, and we'll go home. You'll stay and sleep with me."

He waited with an odd, excessive alertness for her reaction to the news. He drew his lips taught until all his teeth were displayed, crowned by the red carnation in the gap in the middle.

"I don't want to," the girl said.

"Don't you like me?"

"No, it's not that I don't like you; I do."

"Well, then?"

"I don't want to."

The young man rumpled his hair.

"What happened is that you're mad at me because I haven't taken the carnation out of my kisser."

She evinced disappointment that there was nothing left in her glass. The young man pushed his over to her, and the girl sipped a little, suddenly serious. She tapped a crumb with her finger, and gathered it into the palm of her other hand.

"I made a promise when fascism fell that I would spend all New Year's Eve with a carnation in my mouth," he said, softly scratching an ear. "I can go to bed with you, but I wouldn't be able to kiss you nor lick you due to this little problem."

The girl scratched her head. She realized that in the way she was smiling and looking at him now, she had just disappointed him.

"I can't," she said.

The young man paid the bill, emptying out a pocketful of wrinkled bills of small denomination.

They walked along, among the remains of the noisy parade and persistent slogans, separated, in a silence that he accentuated with his head bowed and his hands deep in his pockets. A few yards from the hotel, the girl decided to offer him some consolation: "I have a five-year-old son. He's staying with me in my room."

He kicked at an imaginary ball and shrugged his shoulders. "And your husband, too?"

"No. I'm widowed."

"Well, then?"

They were at the door. She said: "Good night."

He said: "Good night."

And he abruptly turned his back on her.

The last vision the girl had of him was that of his tousled hair merging with the annoying trolley no. 11, Graça. She skillfully took out a cigarette and lit it with a precise flame.

The maid was in her bed reading a romantic story.

"Everything is all right, ma'am," she said in anticipation. "Just perfect."

"He didn't wake up?"

"Not even for a second."

"I don't know how to thank you."

"Please don't mention it, ma'am! Was the plaza nice?"

"Yes," she said.

"Did you walk around a little?"

"Yes."

"A new year, a new life, isn't that right?"

"It was very nice."

The maid yawned spontaneously, and tried to hide it by humming a little tune. The girl unbuttoned her blouse and put her cigarette on the rim of the ashtray.

"What time do you leave on your trip?"

"At ten. Wake me at eight, please."

"Certainly. And where are you going, ma'am?"

"To Romania."

The girl shook the woman's hand in the doorway.

"You've been very kind. I'm grateful."

"See you tomorrow, ma'am."

The maid went down the stairs, and was about to turn off the light in the lobby. She hadn't quite locked the vestibule when she noticed a young man with a carnation in his mouth on the other side of the glass door. Without knocking he indicated with a crooked finger that she should unlatch the door. With curiosity the woman cautiously leaned an ear forward.

"A young lady," the young man said through the glass. "I don't remember her name. The one who has a little boy."

"Yes," the maid said. "The Chilean."

The young man looked at her gravely and blinked profusely. With an awkward brush of his hand, he tried to rearrange the hair that spilled over his forehead, without success.

"Exactly. The Chilean. I have to go up to see her."

"She already went to bed."

"Well, that doesn't matter. Open up."

The maid opened the latch and the young man climbed the first steps.

"Look, she must be asleep."

"What room?" the young man yelled from the second floor.

"Eleven," the maid said, looking up the stairway.

The young man knocked on the door, but didn't wait for anyone to answer. He turned the knob and burst into the room. The girl was naked, except for her panties, which she was on the verge of slipping down over her hips. The young man stepped forward without hesitation and took the flower out of his mouth. He put it in the vase, next to the other carnations. He looked at the girl's small breasts, and stuck his hands back in his pockets. "Well," he said, before leaving the room, "next time, be more explicit."

Setúbal, Portugal, 1975

The Call

The voice caught up with him at the corner of the school, and although he could not discern which of the two men had called him, he sensed they were police. As they approached, he put his right wrist on the pocket where he kept his cigarettes and calculated roughly how many he might have used up during the morning. He had to switch his briefcase and raincoat to free his right hand in order to shake hands with one of them.

In spite of the fact that the young man shook hands with a warmth that went beyond official courtesy, the professor had no doubt about his own intuition.

While he was being subjected to the odd effusiveness of the beardless young man, he tried to pick out some trusted student from among the throngs that were surging through the door of the National Institute. But the mere fact of having displayed that indiscretion showed him he was starting to get confused. As soon as the man released his hand, he was immediately beset by the other individual, who also was perfectly shaven and had some emblem in his lapel.

"Sergeant López," deciphered the younger man, hanging on his gaze, as if this whole act of smiling and shaking hands were some kind of code the professor should already have been able to intuit.

"Gentlemen," he then said, "I was already detained a month and released for lack of evidence."

"Yes, Professor, yes," the beardless young man said in an unconcerned monotone, adding a shade of comprehension to his smile by the emphatic way he used his chin. And in the following silence he held his smile, sharp like a knife, while the sergeant with the emblem crossed his arms and gazed at the traffic on Alameda Avenue.

"Don't you remember me, Professor?"

Furrowing his brow, the professor tried to catch something familiar in that face without features. He pretended to think, and, patting his jacket pocket, he located his glasses, and brought his right hand to his heart with the intention of taking them out. The gesture felt clandestine to him. The sergeant couldn't help taking note of it; and then the teacher said, "My glasses."

Encumbered by his leather briefcase and raincoat, he had to bend over like a cripple to put his glasses on. That way he could once again dwell on the empty features of his interlocutor.

"Come on, Prof," the latter said, encouraging him with a very Italian gesture, "don't make me look bad."

The teacher minutely pinched the orifices of his nose.

"A student, right?" The young man looked gratified at the so-called sergeant and nodded, searching for still more with his eyes. "I would guess by your age that it was in the last five years."

"Exactly. I graduated in '70."

" '70," the professor repeated, disturbed as much by the date as by a certain insinuation in the young man's phrasing. His cheeks were on fire. His face must have been as flushed as if he had choked on some cheap wine. "So many things," he heard himself say incoherently, "you get old and your memory..."

"Fuentes!" the other interrupted him then. "Miguel Angel Fuentes, number 17."

"Of course, Fuentes, Fuentes," murmured the teacher.

"On the exam I had to analyze the poem by Nicanor Parra. You always said you were exactly like that character. The poem about the old professor."

"Ah! Yes, yes, yes! Of course!"

"I was in the class that at the end of the year presented you with the complete works of Neruda. A leather-bound volume on onion-skin paper."

"I remember, of course I remember."

"It was very nice because we all signed the first page, do you remember that?"

"Of course, Fuentes, of course!"

The sergeant also nodded, as if he wanted to testify to the legitimacy of the professor's recollection, but at the same time he was distracted, perhaps wishing to get on one of the buses to the Hippodrome or to Santa Laura Stadium. The teacher noticed his own thick and sticky ankles, as if he were sinking into honeyed asphalt. As the last silence proceeded, twice he was on the verge of holding out his right hand to signal his haste and to bring about the denouement. But on both occasions he was inhibited by the exchange of glances between the sergeant and the beardless man, just as if they were nudging each other lightly with their elbows, sending imperfect signals.

Courtesy became infinite, charged still more with foreboding, blind and imprecise.

"Well," ventured the professor.

"And Neruda died!" Fuentes continued, shaking his head. "Who would have guessed! He was a very good poet, isn't that right, sir?"

"Very good, indeed, very good."

"Nobel prize, too."

The old teacher noticed a warning at the corners of the young man's mouth. I smoked five cigarettes in class and one at break time, he thought. There are fourteen left, just fourteen. He foresaw the technique of the attack. First, weakening the defenses, then probing, then wounding, and at once, finally.... Thirteen, he thought, when the sergeant raised his hand to light it for him.

"I was already detained," the professor exhaled, together with the smoke. "They questioned me. They found no grounds, Fuentes."

"Yes, I know, Professor. How could I not be aware of that when you taught me for a whole year!" He had placed a frank hand on his heart, and with his chin he made a gesture of heavy, ceremonial weight. "It's just a matter of pure routine, you have no cause for alarm. From time to time, the sergeant and I just stroll around here and there. With you, Professor, there is no problem. Isn't that right, Sergeant?"

"There's no problem."

With a sincere look the beardless young man offered him his hand, and when his palm pressed that of the old teacher, he put his left hand over both. Fraternally, in a fraternal way. The sergeant said only, "Pleased to meet you."

Upon crossing the street, the professor transferred his briefcase with his school work to his right arm and dried the sweat from his hands by wiping them on his raincoat.

At the Indianapolis Bar, he squeezed the yellow bakelite token before going to exchange if for a coffee. Absorbed, he moved it around in his fist as if it were a die, and at once he handed a coin to the cashier, his voice sounding hoarse as he asked for a telephone token. He put it into his fist, together with the coffee token and sought out the empty space by the counter right beside the phone. There he hung up his raincoat and set down his briefcase. Although he didn't put sugar in it, he stirred the coffee several times before deciding to taste it. On bringing the cup to his lips, the steam fogged his glasses, and he drank the first sip with his eyelids tightly closed.

When he drew out his handkerchief to clean them, he turned his body slightly to the right, and then he saw the fat man, scarcely three feet from him, with *Ultimas Noticias* opened to the horse-racing page.

He finished rubbing his glasses, raised them against the sunlight that filtered through a discolored, brownish curtain, and further perfected the transparency of one lens by removing a minuscule speck of dust, just below the frame.

Then he downed the rest of his coffee in one gulp, and, since he was absolutely certain that his intuition was infallible, he picked up his raincoat and briefcase. He did not make the call.

Cinderella in San Francisco

So, when Garth Winslow and Suzie Sun got the guitar out of the rickety old wardrobe, and Winslow spat on his hands and tuned the guitar a minute later, playing a pristine E on the first string, and Suzie did nothing but moisten her lips, which the weak American beer flowing between her teeth had dried out, and everything seemed to indicate that all was going well, that Winslow was ready to set the world on its feet and put its heart in the right place, and after singing the blues and some Mexican songs, there was no doubt that he would gracefully enter Suzie Sun's body discharging to the world the love he had accumulated during the peaceful nights of Roble Road in the Berkeley hills, and that he would be well received; I turned to Abby, who was punching holes in a can of that filthy Blue Star beer, and said to her in a perfect, natural English, *all right.* That "all right" told Abby's hand, whose slender fingers were now spread over my hand and whose pressure made me feel how fragile their bones were, that I agreed to go with her to climb the building's service stairway, whose old steps would creak, teasing the peaceful neighbors who were engaged in noisy, syncopated dialogue, as they rested

on their pillows from their affectionate activities.
That's the way we would reach what she called, in a
suggestive voice, "the garret," but which, when we got
there, turned out to be a dirty but adorable attic just
like the one in my aunt's three-storey home in
Santiago. Only here you could see San Francisco Bay,
and, when night was just beginning – a clear San
Francisco night – if you squinted, looking through the
window that you had to clean off with your fingers to
see through, you could also see the string of cars
crossing the bridge that connected the peninsula with
Oakland and Berkeley, where that very afternoon I
had taken a relaxing nap in R. L. Stevenson's home
(presently in ruins and inhabited by flea-bitten dogs
that Renée Deans was nursing with maternal tenderness; the very home of R. L. Stevenson himself, the
filthy pirate whose *Treasure Island* I had devoured
one childhood afternoon in Antofagasta), and it
looked like the movement of stars, or of luminous
lizards, or of giant reptiles, and it did my soul good.
And then that image did my soul harm, because with a
strange intensity I recalled a Mapuche legend that
tells of a child who sees fireflies over the *maqui*
bushes for the first time one night, and then the
second time, he doesn't seem to know what the
restless, luminous flickering means; he doesn't recognize them as fireflies, the daughters of opaque,
subterranean gods. Death will not be long in ensnar-
ing him, and usually it's in a swollen river, with the
floating body hitting against broken branches along
the edge; or perhaps it tells of a deserted house and a
mother, with no expression on her face, waiting
months for her son to come down from the hills, the
son who she knows lies in the gut of a puma that ate

him for lunch without revulsion; or perhaps he's petrified, near the volcano, sculpted in the snow of the majestic mountain that the Lord gave us for a bulwark. And that's what was harming my damned soul, because San Francisco had caught me up in its enigma as a city of death, nourishing its beastly heroism on mystery, on the lights snatched from the enigma by people who love each other silently, without ado, too wise to make a joke   out of life.

I averted my eyes from the bridge and turned toward Abby, who was looking at me intently, perhaps thinking what the hell was going on in my head that made me blink with such a frown, and distractedly stick my fingers up my nose, scratching at the little hairs inside, until I got a few out and wiped them on my trousers. I tried to see if there was a couch, or a rug, or any other soft thing in the room that I could lay Abby on so she wouldn't get dirty when I got on top of her and told her some secret with the breath and joy of physical companionship, destroying myself in greasy, gelatinous drops that would nest in the starry hearth of the planet. But, in fact, there wasn't even a copy of the *Herald Tribune* that we could spread out and do things like a couple of civilized beings would. At the same time I got a tremendous urge to urinate Yankee beer, and it just didn't seem right to do it against the wall in front of Abby, so, with the pretext of some strange need for solitude, offered in an English that not even the devil himself would have understood, I left her, went to the stairwell and urinated like the lord of the manor on each one of the steps. Then, simply to kill time, I rubbed my right foot over the puddles, trying to clean up, just in case. I groped my way downward, feeling the fresh dust on the railing with my hands, and, getting to the landing, I picked up the six-pack of beer I had brought in case we got dry throats. When I got back to the garret, Abby was leaning against the window, with her face turned toward the interior, so that the reflections from outside, from stoplights and neon signs, eliminated her individual traits, and formed only a sketchy outline of her shape. You couldn't tell if it was the same Abby I had left there minutes before, or an eight-year-old girl looking from her infantile world into the cave of the bear, which I looked like, wrapped in my big brown overcoat with its fur collar. However it was, the image it evoked in me, of the perfect prey for the uprooted animal hungry for tenderness, altered my nervous steps, and, opening both arms as if prepared to smother her in a tight embrace, I began to walk toward her, raising my knees and noisily emphasizing my lethargic stride, the way I had once seen bears do in a movie. The girl started to laugh uninhibitedly, putting her fingernails over her mouth, pretending to be frightened, although without moving, making gestures that I could now discern, having adjusted to the darkness. I was silently grateful that she was keeping up this game about the kind of jungle I had established for the purpose of being able first to grab her, as if playing, and then to press my legs against her thighs and kiss her mouth and touch her breasts, just in case any of that turned out. When I was one step away from her, I stopped and beat on my chest with both fists to emphasize the emotion of the moment, accompanying the action with certain grunts, supposedly those of a hungry bear. Then, I approached still closer, and, while she pressed against the wall, I groped with my arms like paws, trying to get a hold of her. Just at that moment she slipped away, and I banged my head on the wall while the girl ran quickly to hide in the opposite corner of the room, mocking the poor animal who, as if crucified, leaned against the wall, sticking his smiling face through the window, looking again at the lights of the cars on the bridge and the immense Hertz Rent-a-Car sign that had been lit up in the distance. Here it became clear to me that the game was taking on two alternatives: I could pursue her through the entire room, growling and jumping around like an efficient bear until I trapped her and threw her to the ground, or, instead, I could stay there, against the window, simulating the weeping of a great but good bear who liked the world but didn't know what the hell to do with it, having not found in a month any quarry who might make it easier for him to do things, and who could share with him her celestial virtues, who might welcome the animal into the starry hearth of the universe, incarnating the monster in his being, freeing him for quite a while from the fucking loneliness that was treating us poor creatures of the Almighty so badly. The image was permeating me, digging in deep, and I felt how all at once my nerves collapsed. In effect, a real feeling of sadness, of a sentimental Chilean, of his daddy's and mommie's little boy, started to displace the boisterous, *macho Chileno;* it started to soften the harsh Castilian words muted in his throat, that he used to curse and praise the universe. Through the muscles in his neck and his barely open chestnut eyes a thing that I damned well knew was sadness was intruding, like a dinosaur in ambush, waiting for just the right instant, the first sign of submission, the heart's first unguarded moment, to

raise its sacred paw and drop him pitilessly. With my
forehead against the window, without making a
gesture, a slow, enormous sadness began to emanate
from the nape of my neck down my back, through the
holes in my coat, from the felt trim on my trousers,
anointed by the grease from the breakdowns of our
'49 Plymouth, seeking Abby's hand, which lurked very
close to my back, as its precise target. If I have any
faith at all in the gods, without doubt the surrendered
gods of silence hoard it all for themselves. They are
the quiet gods who intercede to fashion a terrestrial,
animal, primitive, colloquial language without dialogue, a wounding, attractive language like the limits
of reason, where each particle of the body gives off
signs of a man cooked in the sauce of his own enigma,
who testifies with a slight tremble in the fingers, with
a certain light in the eyes, with a way of falling down
and causing his hair to bristle, with an honest way of
feeling his genitals, with a kind of tremor in his arm
and cheek muscles, their independence displaced,
bathed in one's self. It makes you aware that this
kneecap is yours, and this fibula, and this cartilage,
and these pulsing arteries, and you, listening to their
flow, and to the beating of your blood against your
veins, and the contractions and dilations of your
sphincter, and the touch of saliva charged with the
bitter taste of beer scraping your tonsils, and all the
bluish marvel of your body and of your mind, which
testify to the enigma, wielding your passing anguish
like a ridiculous jewel, your not-so-passing nonsense,
and your honest style of existence, may its greatness
be damned, regretting even what it doesn't have, and
blessed because the sage god of crooked teeth, whose
bittersweet smile appears within the coarse framework

of his mask, transforms you into a magnet, and you attract steel. Everything concludes in you, and it ends in you, brother, and is reborn in you and not a second will pass until you get excited and become immortal, and tell yourself that you're a queer if you let yourself get eaten up, failing to deserve your companion, and failing to deserve the mystery; not until you tell yourself that you shouldn't bear cowardly children either, to work in servile banks or to teach in girls' schools, and that you should force yourself to be the man you are. Not a second will pass until a real manliness, born of defeat, of the footsteps of dinosaurs, a macho sprung from its head and belly puts your two feet on the ground, and you confidently await whatever may come, and you won't get involved with trivia, nor affectation, nor weepy gestures when the arms of a woman encircle you, taking you by the waist and she says to you: Little boy, little boy, what's wrong? in a language that isn't yours, but which you will now speak boastfully, like a Shakespearian actor, because there is nothing in the world you don't know when the moment approaches for the arrival of the angels, and you can respond: Nothing, nothing's wrong with me, and you can say in English what you were thinking, not leaving any words out, speaking with your feet, with your eyebrows, with your tongue chewed between your teeth, with your laughter if you lack the vocabulary to utter at last the only word you can say: I, here, exist.

"Nothing, nothing's wrong, I was just thinking," I said to Abby.

I turned around and took her head between my hands, and caressed her hair and kissed her on the forehead. Then, I put my hand on the back of her neck, and held the same look with which she was pledging me her companionship that night. I had soon enveloped her and was caressing her whole body, and her hands were pressing on my back. Then, I held her apart for a second to take off my beloved overcoat, and, throwing it on the floor, I leaned Abby back on it and I stretched out beside her and we proceeded to caress each other without speaking until I put my hand under her dress and tried to take it off, when, to my surprise, she stopped my maneuver, holding my hand. Paralyzed, I left her alone on her stomach without knowing what to do. As soon as she let up her pressure I resumed caressing her, and this time she let it happen, but when I pulled down on her clothing, she pressed against the floor, making it hard for me.

"Why not?" I asked.

I was very excited, but not angry.

"I don't know," she said. "You're leaving tomorrow for Mexico. We've only known each other for three days. I don't even know how to pronounce your name yet."

"Antonio," I said, getting up and going toward the window, "Antonio."

"Antonio," she said. "Is that right?"

"That's right," I said. "Now you know how to do it."

She sat up on the coat, crossing her legs. With her right hand she caressed the fur, apparently not knowing what to do.

"That's not what I meant to say," she said. "I don't know anything about you. The only thing we've done since we met is sing with the guitar and drink beer. You hardly know who I am. Where are you from? Why did you come to the United States? Why are you here with me? Why aren't you spending tonight with Suzie or Renée Deans, or somebody else? Do you understand?"

Not even if she had analyzed my whole life trying to discover the frail nucleus of my strength in the world; not even if she had spent her entire lovely existence meditating on how to knock me down, on how to tear me apart and put me back into the gloomy speechlessness of bewilderment, could she have done it so well as when that long string of why's emanated from her throat, in that voice I ached to kiss. She only had to ask why I was with her that night and could have left out the rest. But no; she had some very incisive why's hidden away; not even if she had planned to fuck me over, could she have done it so well as with her why this and why that. What did she want me to tell her? Did she want me to tell her the story of my life that night? And what kind of fragmented story was I going to hand her if I didn't tell her chapter and verse the story of my father, and that of my grandfather Esteban, diving into the Adriatic from a second floor on the island of Brac, opposite the port of Split in Yugoslavia, when he was eighteen years old. And what fragmented and still stupider story of my grandfather, if I didn't tell her who my great-grandfather Jorge was, living in a farming village, speaking foreign languages and a few dialects, reading Goethe in German at night and milking cows at dawn, telling *Faust* to the villagers when the occasion would arise to loosen his tongue and finish off the sweet Yugoslavian wine at local gatherings, and about the bowl of gigantic almonds that he would chew on between one story and the next, fortifying himself as he squeezed the guts out of the legend, without great theatricality, while his audience, probably distracted, pulled crumbs off the bread, destroying its celestial leavening, and made tight little balls out of them so they could flick them the length of the table with a finger. As Saturday night would advance and Sunday morning would dawn reddish and fat like a rooster, the sound of bells would fill the air as breakfasts were prepared for the sons who would travel to Split to watch the Sokols or the national team play the Turks or the Romanians. And how could I answer intelligently without talking about my mother Magdalena, who unexpectedly gave birth to me in November of '40 in Antofagasta, and not in Brac, nor in Hiroshima. And how about old Don Cosme, Magdalena's father, who spent his life behind the counter of a moth-eaten general store at the corner of Prat and Esmeralda streets, filling out endless five-hundred-peso forms to get rich by playing the nags at the Antofagasta race track; and about Elena, his wife, knitting socks and sweaters, frying live mackerels jumping happily in the skillet over a coal stove in the kitchen. I would need to know how to respond to why Cosme was with Elena and got her pregnant, why Magdalena accepted Antonio, my father, and cast me into the world. After that, I'd have to know how to respond to why I'm friends with Manuel Silva, Samuel Carvajal, Fernando Vargas, and Jaime Escobedo, and why I got an A in a subject as meaningless as Symbolic Logic, when I went to the University to study philosophy, and why there are people I despise and people I love, and why I've written stories with titles like "Jogging and Tracing a Kind of Parabola with My Right Hand" or "Who is the Master of the World?"; and why I'm a writer and not the Minister of Public Works for the Principality of Monaco, or a homosexual pianist plying his charms in some brothel on Vivaceta street; or a filthy charlatan inventing stories about neurotics and writing for the enjoyment of bearded old ladies, love stories with dirty words and flowered borders; and why I didn't commit suicide when I had a real urge to do it from the tenth story, and I pissed my pants just from looking down, and told myself immediately to cut out the bullshit as I went serenely to bed, and the following day I went to school really early and perfectly absorbed the secret to Carlos Fredes Aliaga's Chilean History class, and then intelligently smoked a Liberty cigarette in the bathroom; and why I can't get the Sea of Antofagasta out of my noggin, or the memory of the lover from Rio de Janeiro; Loco Malbrán and me stretched out on Flamingo Beach talking about Plato, and watching the pigeons fly over the Atlantic, while passionately wanting to go to bed with the two girls lounging in swimsuits ten yards from us; and the marihuana in Panama and the kidney infection that fucked me up for three months and revealed the world to me while my ass peeled off from spending so much time in bed. Why couldn't I give something without talking and talking endlessly about the beloved William Saroyan, and of Saint-John Perse himself, whose book was stuck precisely in my coat pocket, was now withstanding Abby's weight, with her tons of innocent and superficial why's bursting from her, perhaps as a protest against the transience of things and the absence of meaning, and the son of a nutty Chilean who might get into her belly if she weren't careful, and after having said all these things in a minute to myself in my heart, I told her: "I love you, Abby."

Which was the holy truth. Right there I could have begun to swear it to her by all the saints and gods I don't believe in until I used up the entire supply of heavenly things and, prisoner to the most mystical emotion, lean against the wall and go to sleep like a Percheron pony tired of running around without direction. However, I had no need to do so. Abby was looking inquisitively at me trying to weigh the degree of truth in my words. In fixing my gaze on hers, I perceived that I hadn't been too convincing. One uses the word love so often that finally you don't know what you're talking about, and, consequently, you don't know what's being left out, and not even what you do makes any apparent sense. Then, when you perceive what a sleepwalking son-of-a-bitch you are, blind, denied even an inkling of the primitive splendor of the primitive word, giving birth to beings where the light is that bursts like a cheap circus trick (I'm thinking about rabbits and the magician's top hat, and about the multicolored handkerchiefs coming out at a wave of the omnipotent charlatan) that leaves us with our mouths open throughout infancy, that same mouth that the world closes on us until leaving our two lines of teeth gritted together, one against the other, and a distrustful feature on our lips and an ironic smile that replaces the open laughter and the emotion of truth. When that happens, when there is a clean being who knows you, who's incapable of being the kind of charlatan you are, who looks at you, who sees through you and says to you like God on Sinai, I do, I do know you by your name, and says Antonio to you, and it sounds a little like Antounio, and you don't remove your gaze, holding it to bathe yourself in the magic of the pristine, and nothing extraordinary is happening, you couldn't make a dirty movie out of that, nor fabricate a novel with a run of fifty thousand. When that happens, a boy who conquers the world every time he breathes a handful of wind in San Francisco and in Santiago, and in Puerto Montt and in Rancagua, and in Mexico City and Guadalajara, and in New York, and he doesn't know what he's conquering because somehow he has lost the world, has, in some absurd way lost its meaning, if there ever was any meaning, in some cruel way he's managed to avoid having another, the one who holds in his hands the word, the sword and the blessed saliva spread over his dry lips by his tongue, witness your inspiration, and contemplate, *in extasis*, your exhalation, casting out into the world the air generated in your viscera, in your story, in your story of the world, like a dragon puffing out grandfathers such as Jorge and fathers such as Antonio, falling hopefully on some Magdalena or on some Marta, creating the future of history. When that's what happens, somebody with his arms at his sides, removed from the senselessness of the grandiloquent word, is initiating the journey toward his own roots, which are in no other place than right there, beneath the soles of your damned shoes adorned with holes, urine and the remains of cigarette papers, tobacco stuck in mud and sand, ready like a pair of scalpels to be stuck into the earth you're treading, even if that's nothingness, or Santiago on a winter's night, or Frisco in a stinking garret, and never in just one place, except the place the witness provides for your being as it screams, stretches, and shakes off the cancerous blues that had it bewitched, knowing in a passing way that man's own land is never missed, because a man's land is wherever he finds himself, and there's no force on earth capable of making you say that with any other word than love. Only this time I didn't say it, but, instead, picked up a can of beer, which I drank straight down, without breathing, spilling part of it on the floor, with a quiet joy that made my blood rambunctious. Then I took another one, offered it to the girl and sat down, leaning against the wall in front of her, taking a sip from time to time, to have something to keep up my momentum.

"Chile," she said after a while.

At first I didn't know what she meant by that; if she was speaking to me, if she was thinking, or if she just liked the sound, or if she simply had an urge to say something.

"That's right," I said, just in case.

"Chile," she said, raising her right hand and tapping her beer can on the floor.

"Chile," I said, letting my excessive consumption of beer push my head against the wall and leave it there. From there I saw her push her lips out and say: "Chchchile."

"Chile," I said drily.

"Chile," she said, wrinkling her nose and exposing her teeth.

If that's what it was all about, I wasn't going to come up short.

"San Francisco," I let out, making the n's resonate in my nose and entire cerebral cavity, accompanying my voice with a flapping like that of an injured pelican, conciliatory and friendly.

"Son Fronsosco," she said.

"The gorrets of Son Fronsosco are protty and vory good for moking love," I said, seriously.

She held her hand out, and taking hold of me, drew me to her side and let me share a good-sized portion of my coat's fleece lining. I stuck my hand under the back of her neck and we lay there looking at the ceiling.

"What do you do?" she asked.

"What do you mean?"

"What do you do for a living? What do you do in Chile?"

"I want to be a writer," I said.

"Aren't you already?" she asked.

"In a way, yes," I said.

"In what way?" she asked.

"I like life," I responded.

"All of life?"

"All of it."

"Sickness, wars, pain and loneliness, too?"

"In a way, yes."

She kept quiet. I wanted her to keep talking and asking me things so she could see all I had learned about the world, but what she did after a moment was take my head in her hands and kiss me. I surrounded her with my arms and soon was on top of her, kissing her hair and caressing her thighs. Now she wasn't resisting; instead, she was smiling with her eyes wide open, doing her part in the caressing with an audacity which, in spite of the exalted state of my sympathetic nervous system, surprised me. We were getting each other more and more excited, until it seemed there was no alternative to doing things right away, to get rid of the hot, sweaty monster, lying in ambush on our skin. But for some strange reason I didn't take the initiative to resolve the situation. I found it pleasant, and all I wanted to do was prolong it as long as I could, until I could make the situation explode in all its glory. For the first time I was not in a hurry, and although Abby was ready, I stopped all movement, groped in the pocket of the jacket and took out a pack cigarettes, helping myself to one and immediately lighting another one to offer her. The girl was sitting up, arranging her hair, tying up the part in back with a rubber band. Demonstrating an ardent serenity (that's what the poets will think, I told myself), I began blowing smoke rings that rose slowly to the ceiling, undoing themselves in the tepid, unsettled atmosphere that we had created in the room.

"What happened?" Abby asked.

"Nothing," I said. "What's going to happen?"

"I thought you wanted to do it," she said.

"Sure, I want to."

"Well, then?"

"You just wait," I told her.

The girl opened her mouth with surprise. Evidently she didn't understand a thing about what was going on, and although she was staring at me like this, as if looking for an explanation, there was very little I could tell her, because I didn't have the slightest idea what was going on, either. I felt bewildered, happy as a clam, and had an extraordinary urge to make love to her. But there I was, leaning forward, moving my head as if I were keeping time to some song, yearning to hear her speak, to reprimand me, or, what would have seemed even more amusing to me, for her to throw herself on me and make me fulfill my manly duty.

"And you?" I asked. "What do you do?"

"I'm an actress," she said.

"What kind of actress?"

"A theater actress."

"Really? Where do you perform?"

"In a new group. It's experimental theater; theater for children."

"And what are you doing now?"

"*Cinderella*, are you familiar with it?"

"No," I lied. "What's it about?"

While she told me the story about the glass slippers, the clock striking midnight, the pumpkin and mice transformed into a carriage and horses, and Prince Charming, and while she sang to me the magic song of "Bibbidi-bobbidi-boo", I put my head on her thighs and devoted myself to feeling her breath on my face, and to watching her hands as she lifted them from my head to emphasize the dramatic scenes with the ugly stepsisters, speaking in a nasal, twangy voice. As she sang Cinderella's ballad, her hands sweetly descended to rest on my forehead, and then they perused my eyelids during the scene with the elegant ball at the palace. When the story ended, it left a gentle silence in the garret, and a pleasant warmth surrounded us as if we had heated the creaky boards we were lying on simply by chatting.

"What role do you play?" I asked.

"Cinderella," she said.

"Seriously?"

She nodded yes.

"Well," I said, "when's the next performance?"

"Today. In Sacramento, two hundred miles from here. We're a traveling theater.

I jumped up.

"Hell!" I said. "What time do you leave?"

"At six."

I went to the window. It was dawning. A greyish light was beginning to outline the structure of the buildings and the Golden Gate Bridge in the distance.

"Pardon me," I said. "You need to sleep. I didn't know."

"It's okay," she responded, "there's time. We'll be going in my car. We'll go pick up some actors and be on our way to Sacramento. Come here."

I kneeled beside her and we kissed.

"At eight we're leaving for Mexico," I said. "Fernando Vargas and Winslow. Renée Deans and Gastelards are going too. When the performance is over, you could catch a bus to the border. In Mexico we'd get along great. You could learn Spanish, and we could have a good time the way we ought to.

"I can't," she said. "Tuesday we perform in Phoenix, Thursday, in Redlands, and Sunday we go to Los Angeles. We have a contract for quite a while."

"That's too bad," I said. "This could have lasted for a long time."

"Perhaps I'll go to Chile," she said. "You can give me your address. I'll call you on the phone. Do you have a telephone?"

"Yes," I said.

In trying to remember the number, I noticed to my delight that I had totally forgotten it. At the same time, my house, my family, the location of the School of Education where I was studying, all came to mind, but it was like a confused mass, where I couldn't make out details, those same, hateful details which, when recalled all day long in Santiago, had led my feet to a freighter heading for the United States, so I could say *go to hell* to the empty and monotonous life in my country.

"Everything's going just fine, then," I said out loud, although talking to myself. "The whole story could start over again. It really could happen."

"What did you say?" Abby asked.

I had spoken in Spanish. What good would it do to tell her the whole story right then?

"Chile," I said. "I was thinking about Chile."

"Chile," she said. "It's an amusing name. Where is Chile?"

I asked her to get off the jacket so I could get a book out of the inside pocket.

"What's that?" she asked. "A book of yours? Have you already been published?"

"No," I answered. "This is a book by Saint-John Perse. It's called *Anabasis*. I want to show you something."

I looked for a very tightly folded piece of paper that I kept among the pages of the volume, which I hadn't studied since the very night I had left Tocopilla. When I found it, I spread it out on the floor, flattening its whole folded and wrinkled surface with my hands. I gestured for Abby to come closer. We stayed on our knees, strategically placed so the scant light would fall directly on the paper.

"A map," she said. "It's a map of America."

"Agreed," I responded.

I pointed with my finger to a place at the upper edge of the paper, and asked her:

"Do you recognize this?"

"Crazy old San Francisco," she said laughing.

"Pay attention, now," I said.

With my hand open I began to descend slowly, whistling between my teeth, until I got a few thousand miles to the south.

"What's this?" I asked, looking her in the eye.

"Chile," she responded, absolutely sure.

"No," I said. "All this is South America. Now, look closely."

I moved my index finger toward the Pacific coast, and pointed out to her a pile of brown spots that was about ten inches long.

"This is the Andes chain. When I get up in the morning and go to the University, I always see its snow-capped mountains. And even though at times I walk from one block to the next pissed off and with my head down, I can't help but cast a furtive glance toward them, and for a while those glances were enough for me. Right? Okay. Now, tell me, where is Chile on this map?"

Abby looked at me intently and put her hand on my back. Then she tilted her head and contemplated the paper with a meditative face.

"Here," she said, hitting a large, green territory with her fist.

"No, sir," I replied. "That's Argentina. A great country. Look here."

She made a gesture like a sullen child and added:

"Look, Antonio, if the sea is there – she pointed to the blue of the Pacific with her finger – and here is the Andes chain that you see every morning when you walk pissed off through Santiago, and here's Argentina, then Chile is in Argentina, and it has to be this, here."

"No," I replied. "What you're pointing out is Mendoza, an Argentine city."

"Have you ever been there?" she asked.

"Yes," I said.

"And here?" as she pointed to Salta.

"No," I answered.

"Why not?"

"I don't know. Now, watch carefully."

I put the nail of my middle finger on the point of the map that said America, and pulled it down, leaving a fragile crease in the paper, already crumpled from so much hasty use.

"Do you see that?" I asked.

"Yes," she said.

"Chile."

"That!"

"What were you expecting?"

"I don't know. But is that a country? How many people fit in it?"

"Eight million."

"Eight million?"

"And comfortably. That white stuff you see at this point is also Chile. It's called the Antarctic. It's full of snow. There are seals, penguins and some sixty men."

"Have you been there?"

"No," I answered. "Why?"

"It occurred to me you might have been there. You seem to have been to a lot of places."

"Don't believe it," I said. "I'm still a hick. I'm still missing the best part. We're still missing the best part."

" 'We're' still missing?"

"Yes," I responded. "The eight million. We're missing the best."

"Are they sad? Aren't they happy?"

"They are not happy," I said.

"Why not?"

"Because they're never happy."

"Why not?"

"Because they're just beginning, that's why."

"Are you just beginning?"

"For sure," I said. "Look here. Do you see this?
The ocean. How much ocean do you think
there is here?"

"More than in all of California."

"How many times more?"

"Ten times more."

I picked up a beer, drank half of it and handed the
rest to Abby. She turned it away with a gesture; I put
it aside, and we fell back on the jacket. Then we got
undressed, and really did make love, nostalgically and
happily, without separating for a moment, looking at
each other's foreheads, noses and ears, and the fuzz
around our armpits, and I looked at her breasts, and
she looked at my navel and legs, and the hair above
my penis, and we could smell the skin on our cheeks
and backs, and our breath, soaked in the smell of
beer, and the sweat on our waists. We ran our fingers
through each other's hair, and caressed each other's
head vigorously before making love, and more sweetly
later on, singing long, silent odes to chance and to
meaninglessness, and to the passing of what we had
done, whose proximity we sensed nearby as the light
of dawn invaded the garret, as objects showed the
richness of their texture for the first time. Piled in
corners, there were cold, useless pieces of construc-
tion material, rotten pieces of plywood, apple crates
full of obsolete jars and tools, burned-out light bulbs,
bottles covered with wax, greasy wrapping paper,
wood shavings, hardened wax in a container with a
broken handle, spider webs ·in the shape of a fan
hanging from the teardrop lamp, which would inflate
slightly with each puff of the cold air that began with
the dawn. Everything seemed to be in repose, damp,
like forgotten human beings, and we were among

them, covered by the garret's mildewy dust, warmly embracing each other, peacefully mocking the world we belonged to. The slightest movements made us appear newborn, breathing for the first time in the world, forcing ourselves to burst out of that scrap iron that lay in ambush, making no noise, save for the hoarse grunting of our love-making, which, now and again, came from our throats like a sort of questioning among animals of the same species, and were soon swallowed up by the room's brown wallpaper. When the light had already filled the room with a piercing brilliance, and had gone from gray to a pale yellow, Abby thought that it was probably six o'clock, and that the best thing for us to do was go down to the bathroom in the apartment, freshen up with some soap and water, and go pick up the actors who would already be breakfasting on the same morning food whose need we were beginning to notice when our stomachs growled in unison, as we dressed capably and without haste. We shook out our clothes and through the window we tossed the empty cans, which bounced on the pavement in the street, making a hellish racket. I put the map back in the book by Saint-John Perse, at a page where a poem began that went something like "a time of high fortune when the great adventurers of the soul seek passage on the path of men, questioning the entire earth about their era, to know the meaning of that very great disorder..." and I don't remember what other things of the same caliber made me press the book against my cheek and quickly store it in my pocket, and take Abby by the waist and go silently down the stairs.

When we entered the apartment we did it with a certain measured commotion so that if Winslow and

Suzie were going at it, they would at least have time to pull up the sheets or straighten their hair. We knocked on Suzie's bedroom door, and we saw her alone, asleep, with her hand under the pillow, breathing calmly. On the night table there was a note to me from Winslow telling me that he had gone to tell his mother he was going to Mexico, that I should remember that we were leaving at eight in the morning, that he was going to get some money and buy a used tire to take along as a spare, and that Suzie was a very serious matter, and he asked God to bless her, and to bless Abby, and asked me not to let her oversleep while he was taking the car to the garage. While I was reading the message, Abby had gone to the kitchen and reappeared with a couple of apples that we proceeded to chew mercilessly, but not without first bringing them to a shine with the bedspread, turning them into two beautiful, brilliant things. After taking a few bites, she walked toward the mirror, and with a certain awkwardness began working on her hair.

"It's Cinderella's hairdo," she said. "We'll travel in costume. We won't get to Sacramento in time to change at the theater."

I watched her, chewing ceaselessly on the apple, until she had finished, and, picking up a suitcase from which a piece of red satin protruded, she invited me to follow her downstairs, where we got into her car, a '54 Chevrolet, meticulously cared for. She sat behind the wheel and got the car going through the streets of San Francisco, obeying the solitary stoplights as if she weren't in the slightest hurry, as if suddenly she wanted to delay her trip, or to change route, to go to the Mirador at the top of the hill, so we might stay there kissing each other and babbling in torrents the things we still had to say to each other. And now, noticing the sentiments that were starting to take hold of me, I presumed that I would keep quiet, aborted on the Scotch plaid of the Chevrolet's front seat, as the car implacably made its way up Laguna Street, toward Broadway. Suddenly she stopped at a corner and honked the horn twice. A smiling face appeared in the window, and, five seconds later, the same smiling face reappeared, dressed in black mesh, an orange hat and a deep red velvet doublet finished off with golden lace on the sleeves and around the collar. The young man opened his arms as if greeting the world, breathed in air deeply, and held it, inflating his entire costume, then bowed before Abby in a courtly greeting, and walked elegantly toward the car, carrying an overnight bag, and said "Good morning," with an Irish accent, and shook my hand. Humming an Elizabethan ballad, he situated himself in the back seat and gave Abby an address. Further on we picked up two girls dressed in a severe black, who, during a large part of the trip, repeated speeches, without giving them any intonation whatever, while they tried to adjust some cardboard noses as twisted as a fistful of serpents. Abby asked me to come close to her, and whispered a rather conventional phrase of farewell in my ear that caused me to draw back a little annoyed, and immediately to put my arm around her shoulders when I noticed she was trembling as she tried to smile. I told her to keep quiet and not to worry, that life has more twists and turns than an ear, and what kind of Cinderella was she if she was going to get like that every time an animal like me got away from the game. But the truth is, I wasn't very convincing this time either, because I felt an urge to hug her and cry like a loony, but I held firm, and although I didn't put out a single lousy tear, liquid came out of my nose in abundance, but it didn't matter because I just wiped it on my sleeve with an indifferent gesture, and it passed perfectly for a cold.

At the Berkeley Bridge, the road forked and I had to get out to take the route home. I waved to the prince and stepsisters, and walked a few yards along the bridge with Cinderella. We looked at the water beneath our feet, and, between nervous smiles, lit a couple of Camels. Then, hiding behind a pillar, we caressed each other until we blushed, and then the damned prince honked the horn. I accompanied Abby to the car; she got in; put it in first; the vehicle moved slowly, and made the typical sound of being put into second. I watched her put it into third, and watched it a good while longer. Then, I set out on the bridge road in a hurry, to get to Berkeley before eight, and go to Mexico with my friends. Soon I noticed that it was going to be a long walk, and I gestured with my thumb at drivers so they would at least take me a few miles further on, but there wasn't a single son-of-a-bitch who would stop for me, except for a bus that came along behind a jeep that I had asked for help, and it braked noisily, snorting like an ox as its pneumatic doors opened. I jumped in, and a black driver was waiting, offering me a ticket.

"I don't have any money," I said.

I pulled my pockets out and showed him. The black started laughing as if he were the very master of the world, and told me to go ahead and take a comfortable seat, and make myself right at home. I thanked him, and the guy kept laughing the whole way, telling me unintelligible things and glancing at

me from time to time in the rearview mirror,
guffawing harder every time he did it, until he got me
going, as well as a working man sitting behind me,
who started a conversation with the driver between
outbursts of laughter, which just made the driver
laugh all the harder. In the midst of so much
merriment, I, who am more susceptible than Juan
Maula, got to laughing with that laugh that sometimes
gets out of control, expressing satisfaction with the
world, and that state of beatitude shown by the liquid
that runs down the inside of your trousers, and that
you try to avoid by squeezing your muscles, but which
you can't manage, because your entire soul is getting
turned on end, and the only fit thing to do is to call all
that by its right name, and piss with abandon, like an
honest citizen.

Stuck in the Mud

All my lousy life I've crawled about in the mud.

Samuel Beckett, *Waiting for Godot*

I played around with the silver dollar, pressing my thumb on the embossing. For a moment I had the idea of telling the Mexican: "It brings bad luck. The old woman in Biloxi said it brought bad luck." I turned on the faucet and drank water from it, dripping some down my neck.

"It brings bad luck," I said.

The Mexican kicked the crate. Behind it he kept an image of the Virgin of Guadalupe, all faded. I looked back at the table and tried to read the newspaper ad. The Mexican pulled away from the wall and I could see his red shirt soaked to the waist. When I tried to wipe the water off my chin, it was already mixed with sweat. I heard him clear his throat, and instinctively I squeezed the dollar until my fingernails hurt.

"*Hermanito*," the Mexican said to me, "let's be reasonable. Let's talk it over calmly."

With all delicacy he put his hand in the opening, lifted the box, and without taking his eyes off me, pushed it up to the table and sat down with a sigh.

"The first point," he said, trying to appear rational, even though he was mumbling his words, "is that you say it brings bad luck."

By this time, I had changed my mind. I could almost guess the argument that was coming. I said to him:

"I already know the point you're going to make. You're going to say: And what do you call that?"

Mexicocity scratched his temple.

"You're on the right track. What's the answer?"

"I don't know what to call it. But we're fucked."

"Could we be fucked worse?"

"It would be tough."

"Then..."

I pointed out the ad to him.

"There's a problem," I said.

The Mexican came alert with his eyebrows. I felt like drinking more water.

"Here it says 'price according to group.' What's that?"

"It's very easy. There are groups of a, b, c or d, or one, two, three, four. Also Rh negative. They pay better for that because its rare."

"And?"

"If you have Rh negative, they pay you double. It's by the law of supply and demand, understand? But as for you, they'll pay fifteen."

I rubbed my arm.

"How much did they give you?"

"Ten. But I'm Mexican."

"And why would they give me more? I'm Latin, too."

"But you have fair skin. I'm fucked by my skin. If I got myself just a little better tan, I could spend the summer in Harlem."

I scratched an ear.

"They'll figure it out by my accent."

The Mexican stood up.

"You're right," he said. "We're going to have to practice it. Stand up."

I let him take me to the door without resisting.

"Now, you knock, you come up to me and slowly you say: *Ai laik tu sel sam blad.*"

I half-opened the door, took one step into the room and said: "*Ai laik tu sel sam blad.*"

"Perfect. That's all there is to it."

"Wait," I said to him. "Suppose they ask me something. Suppose they ask me what my blood type is."

"You play dumb, *hermanito*, you smile and say: *Ai dont nou.* Let's repeat it all."

I half-opened the door and took a step into the room: "*Ai laik tu sel sam blad.*"

" *Wats yuar grup?*"

"*Ai dont nou.*"

The Mexican started to adjust his tie.

"Put your jacket on. I'll wait for you at the front door."

I put the dollar in my coin pocket, and before tossing on my jacket, I pressed it out with my palms over the mattress. I put a little spit on the old chianti stain, from when the jacket and I knew better days. As I tightened the knot, I felt like the humidity would make me explode at any moment. Whenever I got some money, I would quit buying cigarettes and get a carton of milk instead. You can go into a cafe, and there isn't a single drunk who'll deny you a cigarette. But sometimes it's hard to find anyone who'll treat you to a glass of milk. You feel bad asking for it. It's not the same as a cigarette.

We went out on Tenth Street, and there couldn't

have been more than fifteen loafers around, standing in doorways with cans of beer in their hands. We went to Stuyvesant Place to catch a direct bus.

"Before anything else," I suddenly said, "let's plan our lives."

We kept going, trying to stay in the slender shadow that fell on half the sidewalk.

"We have a few debts," I said to open the topic.

The Mexican nodded.

"Tabs?"

"Excluding restaurants?"

"I think so."

"We owe eight bucks at the store."

"Pay four. It's to our advantage to keep our credit open."

I cleared my throat cheerlessly. Even my stride was choking me.

"That leaves us with eleven."

The Mexican also swallowed hard.

"Eleven," he repeated. And then, only a little more recuperated: "Well, that's something, isn't it?"

I had to admit it was.

"Let's plan it out."

"Rice," Borderboy said. "A little bag of rice is cheap and nourishing."

I had my doubts because all the Chinese I knew were skinny, short and jaundiced. In any case, rice is filling. What we had to avoid after all was that sensation in the stomach that feels like they're pulling all the air out with a string.

"Beans," I added. "They're cheap by the pound. Besides, if we mix the rice with the beans, we'd have something like a real meal, no?"

The Mexican wiped his lips with his wrist.

"You have to have a balanced diet," he decreed. "Even if it hurts to the core, we have to get some sausage."

I swallowed hard.

"Ten, at a *daim* each, makes a dollar. A dollar's worth of beans and a dollar's worth of rice: three. We'll pay four to the store. We have eight left. Eight dollars."

He saw my desolation in the grimace on my mouth, and wiped his nose. He always feigns courage by blowing his nose.

"That's not bad," he said, "considering that we'll be able to eat for two weeks."

"Almost three," I proclaimed. "Twenty days at the ration of half a sausage a day."

We turned sideways as we passed the Martini pizzeria. When he was about to hail a bus, I held him back by the sleeve.

"There's one problem," I said.

"What's going on? That's the bus to Saint Luke's."

"There's a problem. The silver dollar."

"What about it?"

He felt my pocket to verify its existence.

"I was thinking," I said. "Maybe the bus driver won't accept it. Maybe he'll think we're making fun of him. Well, I don't know."

"You're right," Borderboy murmured. "We could save the dollar and go on foot. It's only fifty blocks."

We looked at the cement yards of Stuyvesant Oval, which we now had to cross, and the truth was that in the whole area there wasn't enough shade to cover your fingernails. We took off walking, thinking about one single thing. Thinking about beer.

At twenty blocks the Mexican turned metaphysical.

"How could we have sunk so low?" he asked.

The question surprised me, not so much because it distorted our situation, actually it defined it categorically, but rather because we had never been quite so high that we could sink "so low." For a moment I had the charming suspicion that the Mexican might have had a splendid past. I, too, had had my moment of glory, as they say, but it had been two years before, in Santiago, which wasn't funny.

"What do you mean?" I asked, even pretending to be offended.

Borderboy didn't wipe his nose this time. A sign that a bitter stretch was coming up, worthy of a tango. It was his will that was no longer working. If things were that bad, what difference would a little more or a little less snot on your cheek make?

"Perhaps you've been a lot better off in the past?" I pressed.

"Much better," he agreed gravely. From September to June I had a scholarship. A hundred twenty. They gave me a hundred twenty dollars a month. *Nau finished. Ouver*, man."

All of a sudden a nameless terror assaulted me.

"The rent?" I asked. "It's August, how long has it been since you paid the rent?"

"*Nou problem*," Mexicocityboy said. "The owner, *finished. Ouver*, the owner."

Our conversations usually ended there. I would ask something, he would answer a couple of things, and the topic would be closed. But there were some thirty blocks left, and an uncommon interest in the owner came over me. Before speaking I swirled around a mass of saliva I had collected while I was thinking.

"What do you mean?" I asked. *Nou mor* on the

planet – *gud bai*?"

"*Nou mor*, man. He emigrated."

"How did he die?"

"Stop fucking with me, dammit. He died, and that's all. What do you want to get sentimental for now? You just die."

"Like a tourist," I thought, "from another country, just passing through. Then he goes home."

"But did they squeal on him? Did they stick him with a knife or something?"

The Mexican put his handkerchief under his shirt collar. He brought it out soaked; after that he wrung it out without looking at it, and then tossed it into the air, whipping it between his fingers like he was saying "bye-bye."

"He died of old age," he informed me. "You get the scene, I take it?"

I shook my head.

"What?"

"It's the same as the thousand-dollar question, shit. I learned it in school. The only animal that walks on three legs is man. The old man's cane broke and he smashed his head against the sidewalk. *Ouver*."

I started to whistle "downhill on a roll, illusions gone."

"And our apartment?" I said, finally.

Mexicocityboy rubbed his hands on his trousers.

"Unless they come and tear it down for being a health hazard, you can die in it in the summer of eighty-eight, and you won't have paid a cent. The only thing the cops know about the old man is that his name was Rispieri. Here, no one knows anyone. When you die, you won't have any worries. No worries, truly."

Pity, my friend didn't know what effect his language was having on me. He didn't realize how it was working on my head. I was already seeing myself with a huge syringe sucking my blood out at Saint Luke's, and a blonde nurse, with an apron fitted tightly over her breasts, saying to the doctor: "He's not resisting, doctor. He's going." And the doctor: "Well, let's not waste fresh material. Suck it all out of him, and then take him down to the morgue. Call his relatives on the phone." And the nurse: "It looks like he's not from around here. There's a Meskin waiting for him in the hallway."

"I'm hungry," I said.

"Well, then, the score's tied, man."

He massaged his stomach, and added: "And besides that, could you imagine what a jerk I am? I've fallen a little bit in love."

"Fuck him," I thought.

"Well, really, really pretty, she's not. She's plump, understand?"

"A fatty," I said.

"Well, as far as fat.... Plump. Good character."

"All the fat ones have good character."

"Well, this one isn't fat, man. She's just a little fleshy. Here, too."

He put his hands over his chest.

"And the other?" I asked.

He moved his hands to his belly. There he moved them around on his skin. He was more hungry than in love.

"*It never hapen*," he said. "I left it that I would give her a call, imagine that."

"Imagine that" meant: one *daim* per call, *tri baks* for a movie, *cáple-a-dólars* for a sandwich. He sighed so hard while he was talking that he managed to dry the sweat off my forehead. Let's say there were about fifteen blocks left. I was either turning crazy or romantic:

"I'm hungry," I communicated (romantic). This thing about their taking my blood makes me feel like...I just don't know how (crazy).

"With money you can buy eggs," Borderboy said, but he was thinking about something else. He was thinking about the plump girl he had something going with, but it would never happen. "I've fallen a bit in love."

I operate by contagion. I also had my little love, but it was half spiritual, like artistic. I was in love with... Ella Fitzgerald. I'm a jazz buff. Real heavy. I caught it from the Mexican. I started to sigh scandalously. That night the black singer was opening at Basin Street East, and you had to have a tuxedo or something to get in. I started to whistle, desolate.

"The girl is pretty, you know? Cuban."

I interrupted my melody for five seconds.

"Bring her to the apartment and we'll have a session of the United Nations, what the hell."

"She's Cuban on all sides."

I played the devil's advocate.

"She must be a chicken-shit exile."

The Mexican slapped himself on the butt. It was like he had remembered something important.

"A supporter of Fidel, man. Revolutionary. She came here before all that stuff with Batista."

For a second I had the sensation that my mouth had quit producing saliva. I remembered a lecture that a Chilean expeditionary had given on camels. He had crossed the desert, and camels had something like a water tank. Like a barrel of water, let's say.

"We ought to get out of here," I said.

Borderboy wiped his nose; a sign that he attributed a certain dignity to the *sabyect*.

"What could we do somewhere else?"

We were rounding the corner, and right there was the hospital.

"The same thing as here, blockhead."

"Which is?"

"Exhale air, inhale it, eat, sleep, and good night. We..."

"...who love each other so much..." trilled Mexicali Rose.

"...are fucked. *Ouver*."

For Mexican-Laborer-Who-Works-the-Land the sight of the hospital was like a vision of the eagle perched on crisp bills. Laughter was beginning to come out of him.

"What we have to do..."

"What we have to do," I thought, with a little terror.

"What we have to do is leave," was my friend's judgement.

I blushed, like they do in the cartoons. It hadn't been two weeks that I had gone to see the Consul, brown-nosing him and reading newspapers.

"You're the one who has to make things happen," said Vivaméxico.

With my stomach like an empty collection box, I, the sentimental nationalist, was going to make things happen?

In Saint Luke's there was a black receptionist. We felt better. There's a solidarity among all the fucked-over in New York. Which doesn't keep you from dying from hunger at any moment, for example. Mexicanboy took charge of the blah-blah.

"*Ai want tu sel sam blad*," he said.

"*Wat cólor?*" the black asked, protruding his teeth.

The Mexican came up to me anxiously.

"What's going on?" I asked.

"What color?" he asked. "He's asking what color."

I thought about it a second.

"Calm down," I commanded him. "The darkie here tried to play a little joke on us. Where's your sense of humor, man?"

He smiled, and went up to the black.

"*Red*," he said. "*Ai want tu sel sam blad. Digmi?*"

"Ah, yes," the black exclaimed. "*Régular blad.*"

"*Yes. Régular. Gud yang red blad. Absolutily régular.*"

The black wrote minutely in a big notebook. He wrote down my name, my age (I said 22, just in case), and put down that I hadn't been sick. I kept quiet about the pneumonia. I must have had my blood too fucked up with beer already to be getting finicky now. Behind the counter he ordered a cute black nurse to take charge. Her face looked kind of Latin to me, and I spoke Castilian to her confidentially.

"Do they take a lot out?" I asked.

She turned around, surprised to hear Spanish from me. In reality, I have a face a little bit like a silly gringo sometimes.

"What do you mean, how much? What are you asking me, eh?"

I saw her maneuvering the syringe. She plugged one glass tube into another, and pushed on it until she got air bubbles out of it. And then the girl said something tremendously philosophical that I recorded for history.

"This is our life," she said, "pure bubbles. Along comes a gust of air one day and carries them away."

I cleared my throat with enough racket for a party. I thought about the sound of a bolero I had heard on the beach at Acapulco, while drinking gin and coconut juice, stretched out over a balustrade. At home I had a book by a famous Argentine. Borges was his name. Without further ado I tossed her an abracadabralizing philosophact.

"So great is the vanity of man, and the only thing he's good for is to draw flies."

The mulatto girl smeared the syringe with a wet cotton ball.

"What are you saying?"

I rubbed the fingers of my left hand lightly in front of my eyes.

"Bubbles," I said. And suddenly, whump!

She went to check if the legs of the stretcher were in place.

"Lie down here."

I obeyed her, probing the surface with the same caution as when one steps into the sea slowly, in case the bottom drops off. "What am I doing here?" I asked myself. At this hour I would have been getting out of class at the Conservatory, heading for my old man's apartment, and it would be winter in Santiago, and Mom would have cooked up some pancakes, perhaps it would have rained, and my little brother would be playing soccer in the street with his friends; I could have gotten into a warm bed, turned on my stereo and listened to *Rondeau à la turk* by Brubeck, and then I could have called some chick on the phone.

"What are you?" the girl asked me. "Argentine?"

She had helped me roll up my sleeve.

"I'm Chilean, but write down there that I'm from Dallas, Texas."

She seemed to cheer up.

"I listen to records by Lucho Gatica, do you know him?"

Lucho Gatica was probably toasty warm at home in Mexico, playing with his kids and Mapita Cortés. Or he'd be happily rehearsing something with José Sabre Marroquín's orchestra in the Odeón studios. I had never seen him in my life.

"Lucho Gatica," I murmured. "We're very close friends," I added louder. "Inseparable. Lucho and me."

She began to scrub my arm, and then pinched my skin looking for the vein.

"Do you have a boyfriend?" I asked her.

The chick assented with her eyes, without moving a muscle.

"I don't," I informed her, "I don't have a girlfriend. Not even for show. *Názing.*"

I was disappointed that my friendship with Gatica hadn't turned her on. Somehow I had expected that she would be gentler with the needle if.... And at the moment she was about to stick me, I remembered the days when I had been sick, and they were taking blood from me every little while to send to the lab. It didn't hurt, I remembered that it didn't hurt. It was something else that got me to stick the fingernails of my free hand in my mouth and chew on them. It was that I felt like a whore, pardon the expression.

Pushing my fingers toward my mouth gave me the chance to cover my eyes surreptitiously. Then I massaged my nose. So much the worse: I internalized the pain.

"Relax, man."

I let my body go with a sigh. The girl had what mothers call the hands of an angel. In one try she filled the syringe, and made me hold a piece of cotton on my arm. She went to the table and wrote something on a piece of paper.

"Give this to the black man so he'll pay you."

She spared me the trouble of going after my sport jacket, hanging it on my shoulder.

"Thanks," I said, blushing.

The Mexican stayed at a distance, watching the operation. They paid me fifteen. One ten and *faif backs*. He joined me in the hallway, and we went out on the street. I was still holding the money between my fingers, and my jacket was sliding off my shoulders. Mexicanboy, as solicitous as a mother, put it back in place for me. I showed him the bills.

"*Hermanito*," he said. "You behaved like a hero. Now, let's go to a *dragstore* to have a sandwich."

I threw the cotton on the street, and straightened my arm.

"I'm not hungry," I said.

He wiped his nose on his sleeve. The bread I gave him turned him into a civilized being. He stuffed it in a pocket and hummed something.

"What's wrong with you?" he asked.

There was already a shadow on the left sidewalk. But the humidity wasn't letting up.

"Nothing. Lets go have a sandwich."

We chose an Italian joint where they served spaghetti with lots of cheese and bologna. For five cents more, you got a glass of thin, tasteless chianti.

We sat at the counter to save ourselves a tip.

"*Hermanito*," Borderboy said.

"What?"

He pensively rolled noodles onto his fork. First, he swallowed hard, then stuffed his mouth and chewed everything, nodding like a priest.

"You know what's wrong with us?"

I looked at him suspiciously.

"We're going through a moral crisis."

Looking askance, he checked the effect of his sentence, while he smeared his bread with grated cheese. The Italians provide parmesan cheese free. Putting cheese on his bread was like swiping a sandwich. Tricks of the poor. I imitated him.

"Aha!" I said.

"A powerful moral crisis," he insisted gravely, rubbing his tongue around his gums.

"Hmm."

"A serious crisis... 'Serious,'" he repeated, savoring the word along with the spaghetti.

I looked at myself in the mirror opposite the counter, and decided to straighten my hair.

"Yes," I said.

"We're young, get it? What we need... how can I put this, kid,... is to enjoy ourselves!"

Any day, like in a fairy tale, a bird would land in my hair and build its nest there.

"Right," I said.

Mexicocity licked the corners of his mouth.

"Go out with girls, for example."

"*Yes, oh, yes.*"

"Have a few drinks."

"Right."

"Etcetera."

I finished off the chianti and asked for the bill.

"Let's go home," I said.

The Mexican wrinkled his brow and saw his destiny in the mirror. The wrinkle in his dark skin turned sad. Like that of a puppy, let's say.

"María," he recited. "María works at Macy's."

I looked at him unperturbed.

"She has a friend, Julie."

"Gringa."

"Nice, brunette, the way you like them."

I took the bill. Without making a big deal out of it, I took out a dollar twenty.

"Does she speak Spanish?"

"Well, that's just a detail, man."

"Does she speak Spanish?" I insisted.

He pensively twisted the hair on his sideburns.

"I gotta be honest with you," he declared.

I propped an elbow on the counter and puckered my lips opposite my image.

Then, something happened that didn't have to happen at that moment. A teenager had put a coin in the Wurlitzer and "Downtown," by Petula Clark, started to play. That week there were two songs that just drove me nuts. The other one was "King of the Road," by Roger Miller.

"You're right," I said. "We need to enjoy ourselves."

The chicks would leave the store at six. It was I, myself, like someone who didn't care one way or the other, who went to the corner to hail a cab. With a tremendous intuition, the Mexican spent the whole trip softly whistling the tune. That really fired me up.

We got some Chesterfields from the machine in the store, and smoked them like Broadway stars, half

closing our eyes and spitting little specks of tobacco
with the tips of our tongues. We crushed the butts
before getting on the escalator, and Borderboy deftly
headed toward the toy section.

Well, now, since it wasn't Christmas or anything
like that, the only people in that section were a couple
of wealthy old Argentines, buying a little electric train
for their grandchildren. When María noticed us, all
her color went right to her cheeks. There was no
doubt that Borderboy was in business. She gestured
for us to go off toward the children's record section,
and make like a couple of nerds looking for *Cinderella* by Mary Poppins, or something like that. I
glanced at the other clerk, who smiled when we made
eye contact. Who knows why. It was God's will, I
suppose. But she was as blonde as Budweiser beer,
with a waist that wasn't at all bad, and big teeth. What
I mean is that if you hadn't seen her before, and you
ran across her in the street, you would guess that she
probably worked in a toy store.

"Do you know her?" I elbowed the Mexican, who
was already finishing another Chesterfield.

He raised his eyes from the records and looked
down again discreetly.

"Julie," he said, swallowing with difficulty.

I began to breathe harder.

"She doesn't speak Spanish, isn't that what you
said?"

He blinded himself exhaling a mouthful of smoke,
looking down.

"Not for shit."

I swallowed about a quart of saliva, and, making a
terrible noise, I cracked my neck desperately. This
time there was no alternative: I was in love with Julie,

and besides, I was a big asshole. I put one hand ove
my heart and massaged it intensely, out of air, feelin₉
trouble between my legs, and, one by one, I took th₎
fingers of both hands and squeezed them until all th₎
knuckles cracked.

"*Luk!*" I advised the Mexican, trying to look
interested in *The Singing Whale*.

María and Julie came to stand right under our
noses. They had a nice smell of pine soap or
something. They had recently washed, and both of
them used a pretty thick layer of make-up. The only
thing I had to do was delay reaching my boiling point
as long as possible, and smile, nodding; it was a
question of either looking cool or like an idiot. But
suddenly I got it; I caught it on the fly, you might say.
Just at the moment I had to smile, open my chops and
murmur so no one in the world could hear me say *plis
tu mit yu*, the light turned on for me, man. I stuck my
jaw out slightly, and without further ado, I looked
straight into the depths of her eyes, and to the depths
of everything that has depth, and telling her everything in Chilean, but only with my look. Such stuff as
"pretty little thing," "my little love," "look how much
I adore you, my love." Something must have happened then, because it was the first time in the history
of the world that a Gringa looked down when she said
hau duyudú.

The blonde was like that, radiant and warm. That
type of girl who always seems to be just getting out of
bed, and it makes you feel like jumping into the warm
bed she's just left and rub your nose on the pillow,
sighing.

Mr Nights of Mazatlán wasn't doing anything much
different with María. They were just talking about I

don't know what shit, but with big parentheses of
silence. The blonde didn't know what to do with
herself, so she *spikt in inglish*, suddenly.

" *Wat yur neim?*" she asked.

"Fernando," I answered without blinking, and in a
deep voice with an insinuation that meant "I desperately need you."

"Fernando," she said, looking me in the eye, and
then began studying her shoes.

"*Ai sed 'yes'.* "

"*Mai neim is* Julie," she then said, looking at me a
little above the eyes, around my forehead.

"*Ai laikit,*" I conceded. And so as not to appear
inhuman, I made a face that could have the flavor of a
smile, should the occasion arise.

María turned toward me and started straightening
the collar on my shirt. Unfortunately; it was like a real
pigsty, as Borderboy would say.

"Where do you want to go?" she asked.

It was nice to feel the fingernails of a little lady
rubbing your neck. Mexican advised me with a glance
that I shouldn't be in a hurry.

"If it doesn't seem like a bad idea," he said then,
"maybe we could go dancing?"

I looked at Julie, hoping to affect her in the same
place I had before.

"No," I said.

" *Wat's rong?*"

"You mention dancing, but you're forgetting,
man..."

"What do you mean, I'm forgetting. What am I
forgetting?" I pointed to my arm with a finger to see
if he would catch on. With my hand stuck to my thigh,
I made a gesture of *money*. "At the dance hall they

have the air conditioner turned off, and they don't
serve booze," I added. "We could..."

I almost cried when it struck me. That matter they
call conscience told me: "Go on, straight ahead."

"We could...?" the Mexican invited me to finish.

I took a Chesterfield from him, trying to keep my
hand from trembling.

"We could," I said slowly, "go to Basin Street East
to hear Ella Fitzgerald."

The chicks consulted each other, with their heads
together, and Mexican began to scratch his middle
front tooth.

María shook her hair, tossing it on one shoulder.

"We'd have to change clothes," she said. "It's a
fancy place, you know?"

"Let's just go like this. It's fancy, but dark. You just
tell Julie to order the drinks in English, and that's all
we need."

The Mexican put his arm around María's waist, and
moved forward a little. Only thing was, his walk had
started to look like a crab's. His legs weren't
responding to him.

"Man," he said to me, "you must know..."

"And God, too," I replied.

As soon as we left the store, I put my arm around
Julie's shoulders, and the chick made a gesture like
someone who's going to lean her hair on your chest,
and New York was just one big mess, and I liked the
situation, and started to hum "Downtown," and my
legs had gotten elastic, like a dancer's. When Julie
started talking with me, I even understood what she
was saying. That is, my body understood what she was
saying. I even tried *sam inglish* haltingly, waving my
arms like the blades of a windmill, and the four of us

had an extended and rowdy walk; we didn't pass a single pedestrian without banging into him properly.

We were killing time until eight, going after the Scotch in an Irish bar, and the chicks had bought some peanuts from a roving vendor, and we were dropping the shells all over the place. Finally it became clear that Julie would be a dancer, and that with time I could play the trumpet in some small-town jazz club. She had a gambler uncle who at some point had made a fortune betting on the harness races in Yonkers, and I had a frustrated inclination toward gambling. As we were beginning our second drink, we started to put coins in the Wurlitzer and to cuddle up in a dark corner. I began to say sweet nothings to my blonde, and María translated, and sometimes the Mexican translated, and he added things on his own, although all of a sudden his tongue got away from him and he turned poetic on me.

By eight we had finished off the peanuts in a taxi, and we were going down the stairs at Basin Street East, with the air of big shots. It was the cocktail hour and at nearly every table there were big-busted dolls with fantastic cleavages. The waiter was tugging us along, and installed us at a second- or third-class table behind a balustrade.

Besides us, there were two silent blacks who would take a sip of whiskey from time to time, and were the only ones in the place not holding cigarettes between their fingers. I thought they must be singers. They never smoke, and they take their drinks without ice. On a platform, a trio directed by a pianist with greying hair was improvising on Cole Porter tunes, à la Liberace, but not as queer. Julie had picked out a corpulent writer, with an injured eye and his skull covered with curls. She said she had seen him on the cover of a magazine, and his name was Norman Mailer, and he was a weirdo. She said that once he had stabbed his mistress. I told the Mexican to inform Julie that I had read a book by a North American named Saroyan, and to ask her if he had ever been on the cover of a magazine, and the Mexican said that Julie said no, but that on another magazine there was a picture of a choreographer named Joffrey, and that she would like to study dance with him. Finally, a midget came out on stage, and the Liberace guy went off to the bathroom with his musicians, and they crowned the midget's silver mane with a rose-colored spotlight. He said he was very *praud* to introduce Miss Ella Fitzgerald, and meanwhile, a trio of whites began in pizzicato to play "Stompin' at the Savoy." Suddenly, Miss Fitzgerald came out all dolled up, and I proceeded to reward myself with half the contents of my glass. Julie, María and Mexicali Rose applauded, less discreetly than the rest of the clientele. From there on for half an hour the nightclub was filled with warbling, murmuring, roller coasters, swings, acts of love, electricity, laughter that rose like birds and burst against bottles, and the ample bosom of Miss Fitzgerald was imperceptibly consuming the air in the place until you couldn't find a way to pump even a little oxygen into your own lungs. You couldn't see how nor by what right you existed on the same planet with that woman; you were the same as a chair, or as a broken clock in front of her; you were just a sad thing with burning cheeks, and solely because She existed, Borderboy existed, and María and Julie, and my parents in Santiago, and the writer with curls, and the book I had read by Saroyan, and the choreographer, and Macy's department stores, and all the blood and hospices; and because she existed people were dying and there were millionaires, and it was good to drink until you passed out, and the black songstress was singing "Love for Sale."

Suddenly, everything was brought down to a simple form. She went into that bathroom, the midget came out on stage, and said *taim tu dans*. Once again it was Liberace with the gray hair and delicate hands, the black bass player, the drummer going cha-cha with his brushes, and the bosomy women lit more cigarettes, and the men snapped their fingers requesting the bill, and then the room emptied out, and the dinner crowd began to arrive. I got out the twelve dollars, handed them to the waiter, and this time I didn't put my arm around Julie's shoulders. This time, I squeezed her by the waist, dropped my cheek onto her head, and we went out to the street.

We walked some eight blocks until what had to happen, sooner or later, happened. What had to happen was that the Mexican would stop to wait on us, and then would say "well..."

I took out the last Chesterfield, and crumpled the package with my left hand. That was the city and the end of it. There were formidable works playing on Broadway, elegant bars to while away the sleepless night, buses that people were getting on to visit friends, jazz at the Village Vanguard, elegant hotels where you could make love, furious and entertaining writers, Latin American painters with scholarships, marihuana at a dollar a joint, museums, a zoo on Broadway, television programs with Ben Gazzara, Puerto Rican parties, night races in Yonkers, cars, and people everywhere.

"Well, well, well," the Mexican said.

I smiled, sticking my hands into my pockets.

Borderboy straightened the knot on his tie.

"I'll go take María home," he announced.

I felt for the coins in my pocket. At the absolute most there was about seventy cents. Subway for two, thirty. Subway for one on the way back, fifteen. Assets left: 25 cents.

"Perfect," I said. "Just perfect."

Julie had me by the waist.

"*Hee'l teik ker of yu,*" María told her.

They went down the stairs to the subway and left us there like two more mailboxes on the street, like two advertisements. Like two spigots of shit, that's how they left us.

"Well," I said.

I took out the coins and looked at them under the street lamp. Eighty cents and no more. I could invest what was left over in coffee. In two coffees standing on the counter in a bar.

"*Wan cofi?*" I asked her.

The chick looked me in the eye. She softly shrugged her shoulders.

I turned my head around to see if there was anything else I could offer her. In Santiago it would have been simpler. I would have said, "Let's go to my place," and the chick would have said, "No, take me home." But here you had to be defeated in English. I even lacked the chips needed to place the minimum bet.

"*Mai houm?*" I said, ridiculously, pointing toward the Hudson River.

The girl started looking at her shoes.

"*Mai houm?*" I insisted, desperately flapping my

elbows, with my mouth dry. My mouth was trembling. There wasn't enough wind even to drag along a candy wrapper.

I urgently needed someone to get me out of this movie I had gotten into. Would somebody please change the stage setting for me. Would someone give me a prompter to whisper Shakespearian poetry in my ear. I swallowed hard.

"*Vamos*," the girl said. She said it just like that, in Spanish.

I spent the trip on the express subway memorizing the advertising posters. Fortunately I had a few loose peanuts in my jacket pocket, and I could offer them to her. We nibbled on them with the tips of our teeth, to see if we could make each one last from one station to the next. By the second peanut, I inaugurated the practice of taking off the red hull, and shaking it off my fingers interminably. And after the last nut, I began to chew on the shells. We were sitting on the wicker seats in the middle of the car, and we didn't matter to anyone. I started humming "Downtown," and the chick took a handkerchief out of her purse, and, with gestures, asked me to help her tie it on. Then she smiled at me like in a shitty romantic movie with Gregory Peck and Audrey Hepburn. And it wasn't that the scene was so rotten bad or anything like that, but, rather, that I was supposed to say something tremendous along the lines of *ai lav yu madli*, and the hell of it was that I wasn't in character. Besides that, for some time I had been suspecting that this wasn't a Technicolor musical that would end with Doris Day pregnant in a suburban home, a job that pays a thousand dollars a month, and blond-haired, blue-eyed children. Instead, it would be one of those modern Italian ones where everything ends with the very worst shit, and the guys go off down some cobble-stoned side street, on a cloudy day, smoking a cigarette butt and dying from the cold.

Our apartment had just one advantage compared with the others in the neighborhood. It didn't smell so much like urine nor dishwasher soap as it did like the paint or thinner from things the Mexican was working on. He had taken to doing colored boxes that some day the Museum of Modern Art, or some millionaire philanthropist would buy from him. I moved around like a bat in the dark, and before twisting the lightbulb on, I threw my Indian poncho over my gray sheets. In a movie, the hero would have delicately pulled on a Chinese lamp with indirect lighting, and would have gotten out ice cubes and a fabulous bottle. To ease my nerves, I started whistling "Downtown." I just turned on the light. What else was I going to do?

The chick blinked in front of the bare bulb, and she looked pink and clean. I smiled as if to beg her pardon for standing there with my stupid hands stuffed in my pockets. After that, I felt jealous of the Mexican, because she approached his boxes and said *biutiful*. My only thing of interest was my brass trumpet above the bed, but any two-bit soldier could blow it better than I could. Besides, Herb Alpert's band was getting popular, and there wasn't even a teenager who couldn't tell the difference between any old braying and music. For a moment, I even thought she had come here because she was as drunk as if she had been at an Irish wake.

I sat on the bed, resting my head on the wall. She got rid of her handkerchief and came to sit beside me. I put my arm around her shoulders, and started looking at the wall. I felt my legs trembling and my lips cracked. I started to sweat like a chicken on the spit.

Then I moved my mouth close to her cheek, and put it over her lips, and with my tongue I tasted the flavor of her sweaty skin. I noticed that the chick was softly pulling one of my hands to her hip, and that she was sticking her warm tongue between her lips and then was licking my left earlobe, and then my temple, and after that she licked her way across my face, and moved down to lick my chest hairs, while I was getting my hand wet between her hot thighs.

" *Weit*," she said in a whisper. She pulled off her panties and bra, and kneeling on the poncho, put her small breasts near my lips. When I leaned over to kiss them, to put my nose in the warm cavity they formed, she started to kiss my hair and forehead.

Slowly I got the whole picture. It was fantastic. We were licking each other.

"*Ai felt sou lounly,*" Julie said, going over my naked back with her mouth full of saliva. I had my eyes closed, feeling for her belly, to kiss it. I wrapped around her waist, and we ended up with our faces on the pillows, looking at each other.

"I understood what you said," I told her, squeezing the back of her neck. "You said you felt lonely. Do you understand me?"

She assented with her eyelashes and a smile. Tender, but hot, too.

"Now you're with me," I told her, stressing my chest with my chin. I held her breasts and put my knee between her legs. "Do you understand?"

"Yes," she responded.

"You can stay here all night."

"Yes."

I slowly pushed my organ between her legs and penetrated her. Everything was fine: the smell of paint thinner, Borderboy's boxes, the roughness of the poncho.

That's when we really did make love. At first, we moved almost imperceptibly, as if exchanging Christmas gifts, souvenirs, she slowly panting, I, mute.

Then I pulled on the lamp cord, and we caressed each other until we fell asleep. Before that, I learned a lot about her back, her thighs, and the smooth rhythm to the curve of her backside. She had touched my legs insistently. And, my jaw.

When I awoke, the light had pierced the sheets of newspaper that covered our only window. Everything in the room was in its usual disarray: the trumpet to one side of the pillow, the Mexican's boxes strewn over the floor, Julie's hand, limp on my hip. I silently straightened up, and smiled as I put on my trousers. I took the silver dollar out of my coin pocket, and gambled my fate on a coin toss. I separated my palms and studied the coin almost without attributing importance to the result. Combing my mop against the window, I moistened my lips with my tongue. Then I buttoned my shirt and went out on the street.

I bought a carton of milk, a loaf of French bread, the end of which I nibbled off, and two tea bags. I invested the change in a plastic container of peach jam. It was going to be a hotter day than yesterday: even the birds appeared stupefied.

Julie woke up when I stumbled in the doorway. She watched me watching her and covered herself to her eyebrows with the poncho. I went to the kitchenette and put the milk on to boil, contemplating the flame. I meticulously rinsed off our only two cups, and smeared jam on slices of bread in silence. Although I wasn't watching, I could sense how Julie was putting on each article of her clothing.

We sat on the bed, and savored the hot, sweet milk, without talking. Then Julie took her purse, arranged her hair over her forehead, spreading it lightly with her fingers, and cleared her throat before speaking.

"*Work*," she said.

I got up to open the door for her.

"Your house," I said to her.

And I pointed at the walls, which were cracked from the humidity.

I watched her move away toward the subway entrance, and at once I sat down on a bench to look at the buildings across the street. I still had a piece of French bread in my hand, and the abundant jam was dripping off the edges. I tossed it in my mouth, and spent a long time chewing it, until I felt it pass down my throat and settle at the bottom of my stomach.

Watch Where the Wolf Is Going

Aye, Captain Sir, I remember; it was a giddy day, the corn was ripe, and the shafts of wheat stood tall. And the sky? Smooth, wide, it scratched your throat. A good day to eye the birds, to break up a trail of ants with a blade of grass; to close your eyes, to open them, get dizzy from the light, from the blinking of your eyelashes, and if you liked, it took no effort to lose yourself in a game of nine pins, but with stones. From the space of that deep and fresh recess, I have forgot nothing. Nor of the sweet young wine, nor of the surface of the sown plots, nor of the irrigation ditch that split their pattern with such a slender line. And it was December in that year of our Lord, and if others were scratching their hands, and gold dust was breaking their fingernails, Alonso de Torres had no illusions.

I took pleasure in listening to the soldiers and scriveners as they longed for Castile. I never had a loose tongue, but the wine on those temperate nights at least turned your ears receptive. The loveliest plans were made around the blacksmith's anvil. It was a sight to behold the thick necks of the soldiers nostalgically bowed over the forge while native lackeys laughed in distant groups, squeezing the tender corn until the juice came out. The guards joined us for the second toast, and wet their lips in the coarse, dark liquid that we kept in barrels. Marín was making plans (more than a thousand pesos to deal in silk), and Pinel was getting thinner; but if day's end reached us, faded and sleepy, our nightly conversations put fire in our eyes, dreams bathed our cheeks (to adorn our daughters with jewels so as to marry them off to proper gentlemen; for the wind is blowing and the women of this century mature young). Sometimes the sun would burst over the mountains, and then the dreaming would cease, voices would pale and retreat inward, and there would be only three or four of us, and we would look at each other and say "do you remember?" Dawn would greet us with the sound of chickens, horses trotting, stony plains, the silence of that mysterious land in violet hues, as we knelt by the dying fire, Captain Sir.

And that day we weren't even talking. Five years among the same few faces can exhaust your lips; we knew each others' smell, our future, the exact nerve that would make us angry. By day we would avoid each other; I had no illusions, but I knew how to share silence. I had become accustomed to the rocks, to turning my best side toward the wind, to laughing louder than necessary. It was at night that we knew how to take each other by surprise, Gaspar Villarroel with his big teeth, a song by Diego de Oro, Vicencio de Monte with his sonnets. That's the way night is for the animals: they seek out the fire, curled up together cooing to each other, lying to each other. They triumph. Later there will be plenty of daylight to restore equilibrium, great mountains to consecrate defeat, all kinds of birds to watch them. I knew, Captain Sir; I knew what death was, in my stomach, in my neck, in the meals of wheat we ate for breakfast, in the irrigation ditches, I knew that this was the land of our death. Others preferred Spain. As for myself, I don't know how else to say it, but I had no illusions. Perhaps gallop some day to Valparaíso, throw in a line to tempt the fish, bathe in those seas I hardly remembered. And that Friday had a delightful air, and early in the afternoon, with a sliver of moon showing diffusely, I recall seeing Juan Pinel, wrapped in his cape, leaning against a tree in that corner, gesturing to me. I thought he wanted to read me one of his letters; he was always writing long letters as if some time a ship were going to leave that would take them away. I can still see him today, running, smothered and tripping on the folds of his cape, with the sun lighting up his cheeks.

"Alonso," he said, "let's quick go to the governor's house."

Unwillingly I bent over my knees. Everyone was running toward the center from the walls of the compound.

"What's going on?"

"The governor has given anyone who wants to, permission to leave on the *Santiago*.

I'm not a man who maneuvers abruptly. I need time to imagine what's being said to me. My responses are slow in coming, and sometimes I laugh at a joke told at a gathering, later, in the solitary silence of my tent. Besides that, I'm somewhat like these rocks (old friends in Spain and a widowed mother). Maybe that's why it didn't seem very important. We went walking along and Pinel had his arm around me, and, coughing from his agitation, he was almost trotting. I grabbed him by the arm; I knew this man was sick.

In Don Pedro's yard no one was missing. Even the guards, with their faces toward the plaza, looked curious. Such care was one of Don Pedro's vices. It was the Indians who were now working the veins of gold, sowing the fields, and sweating from sun-up to sunset at harvest time. I liked to see those radiant fields, with their bushels of wheat, and in April and May, when the corn is gathered. We had done everything with a couple of ears. Those were days when for dinner we would have chicken, suckling pig, fresh eggs from nearly a hundred laying hens. If it hadn't been for that meeting that December day, I would have forgotten about Spain. Those weren't the sterile times of '41, when one had to chew on the seeds from our plantings and onion bulbs toasted in hot sand, or chew on the kernels of small grains like oats, and when one didn't husk the wheat so as to conserve its juice, and the Indian women were capable of biting into your jugular when you mounted them. Jofré still carries teeth marks, although the woman died rotting at the bottom of a ditch. These were good months. If you wanted gold, you just got an Indian lackey to scratch out your part of the mine; if you had no illusions, you could get away safely among the veins of the hills and invent music with your trumpet. I tell you, Captain Sir, to revive hope in a wise man who has killed off hope is to murder him again. But I'm not speaking on my own behalf. I'm protesting on behalf of Pinel's wife, of my friend's letters, of Marín's children, because not even the Indians were that treacherous.

Yes, I'll be frank. Allow me to loosen my tongue

with this red wine, for rage is growing in me as if it were once again December.

It was the governor himself who spoke. He was smiling. He said that we could buy our passage on the *Santiago,* pack out our gold, and once in Peru it wouldn't be difficult to head for Spain. That warmed the blood of all the lads. They had lost all memory of this same man's proclamations to the effect that no one would abandon this land before dying. Only the favorites didn't raise their hands. Of course, they had the land grants, the allotments of Indians, a seat at the table of Don Pedro himself. Pinel held his hand up almost all afternoon; if someone came up to make fun of him, he would say: this hand for blonde Isabel, this hand for Juana, and he would bite his wrists, and would stretch out on the ground with his hand over his heart, trying to hold in check its beating.

And that's where the party started. The vintage wines came out, the pig went on the brazier, I provided music from early in the afternoon, and Núñez accompanied me on his instrument. Laughter grew like a rain storm, and throats got hoarse. Pinel kept looking for a corner where he could softly cry. Even Don Pedro came around celebrating with his favorites from the plaza.

Don Pedro had to cut the party short; a lot of wood was squandered on the bonfires, and the lookouts reported groups of curious Indians prowling around the fort. I got ready to leave in the early morning. Why sleep? When I get started on music, the melodies just won't quit. If the troops applaud, melodies take after me like starving gulls, they attack my head, and I hear the sound of choruses for a week. I didn't even join the gang that went out to roam the countryside. And at that, I liked the women, the aroma of their breasts, the cracked skin of their knuckles, their hips, which would break loose like a colt if your fingers knew how to make the right tender moves. I was never like the others, who fornicated with disgust. More than one night I shared sugar, bread and bed with one of those silent women in my tent. Once I talked with one of them. I talked to her in Spanish, and the bitch appeared to understand, and smiled, naked, eating a plate of beans by the light of the fire. If you want me to tell it straight out, I had nothing to celebrate. For that, the stars of this land and the night, scrambled by breezes and so many kinds of silence, and the Andes, sufficed. That was my blessing and my farewell. To set out on my way without fanfare, without music, without words. I'm telling you no lie when I say I slept that night with my ear to the ground listening for the arrival of dawn. One listens to the light of these mountains, Captain Sir.

I was the first to leave for Valparaíso. I tied my shirts to the back of my mule and set forth crossing the hills without haste. One last time I wanted to savor the early morning breeze, anticipate my old Spanish friends, trace the patter in their mind of Madrid's cobbled streets. That Saturday started in fog, and at the edge of the furthest rise I stopped to greet the shouts of the lookouts with a wave. As soon as I got on the flats, I started to trot, and the mule, breathing heavily, got to galloping, and the Indians meekly fell back when they sensed our steps. I had never thought I would see the ocean again. During the destruction of Santiago I had caught a spear in the leg, and I thought the fever would kill me. Some woman tied up my thigh with my breeches, and before passing out, I thought I saw the sea vanish. Not this Pacific we're looking at now, but that powerful, luminous sea of the African coast, where I had spent my childhood. And in my dream the sea swirled, it got rough, passed over the nape of my neck, covered the sky with foam; and I heard my father's voice, casting his breath against my ears: It's a sign you're dying, Alonso; pray now, pray. It was for that reason, because there was that greenish, motionless sea everywhere, and because my lungs yearned so cleanly for the air, that I squeezed the medallion of Santiago between my fingers and went down to the beach praying, not from fear of death, but from being so strong, so solitary and content, and so hungry.

It didn't take me long to notice the vessel bobbing off the rocks of Cabo Santo. The crew came out, and I gestured to them that shortly I would be coming aboard. I untied my bundle, tied the mule to a stone, and looked for a good rock from which I could cast my line. That was a good lure, Captain Sir. We had rounded it to a point, hammering it in the forge and I spent sleepless nights or my turn at guard sharpening it slowly against a piece of rough metal. Even the bait was first-class: noisy chunks of *piure* mollusk that let out a spurt when you stuck in your knife seeking the heart of the meat. I spent an hour noticing how the salt soaked into my beard. A full hour without anyone daring to disturb the balanced flight of the birds. And even though the fish shunned the lure like it was the devil himself, it didn't matter to me. I would have occasion to test the virtues of that gold hook on the high seas under a full moon. You'll have to forgive me for still bragging about these things. Only one fish took my bait, and probably because it was little, awkward and inedible. I calmly unhooked it, and threw it back in the water. It was around dusk, and the stream of wine from the bota turned golden with the tone of the twilight along the length of its course.

And later, along the edge of the mountain, stupendous, graceful, drifting in a fantastic remoteness, the rest of the travelers descended, and their capes waved black against the pallid texture of the open fields. I got on my mule and we set out at a slow pace to meet them. All the way along I was guessing by their mounts who was in the lead. Soon, I figured out from his sorrel and helmet that Don Pedro was leading them. Like laughter from the sea their voices were carried to me. The stragglers pressed the haunches of their mounts, and even the oldest cut loose rolling on the sands, and shouting Eehaw, away with Alonso Torres and his sainted mother. They unsaddled at the edge of the water, and the youngest ones jumped right in, far enough to get covered by the waves.

Later that night we made bonfires, and soon the jugs were circulating, pouring into the gullets of the voyagers. The youngest ones, already drunk, rode their horses barebacked on the beach, and if the ponies bucked them onto the sand, they would roll into the water and then dry themselves by the heat of the summer stars, and of the moon, or they would down some wine by the fire. I couldn't help breaking out my instrument, and we sang and danced in our bare feet, and the boys bruised their palms clapping, and the veins on their necks stood out. Alonso Aguilera and Bartolomé Díaz got themselves swords and right then the party heated up, and it was something to watch those two warlocks with the music of their blades carve up their rivalry by sheer dint of feinting and laughter. Obese in their armor, with sweat running down through their beards, they spat and cursed just as if they were not the best friends in the world. I didn't know which was the greater enchantment: the sea bursting into foam virtually over our faces, or the clanging of the weapons, or the greatest happiness among a gathering of men that I had ever seen in América. I would give my right arm, Captain Sir, just to live that night over again sometime. And then the crew of the ship showed up, and the merchants began to check the mouths of the horses, and examine their hooves; someone even made me an offer for my trumpet. But why would I sell it! The only thing I wanted to do was to make it shine some night in the very knot of the waves when the sails had been set to cruise against the moon and the wind. I planned to make a bird out of my trumpet, to rip the night open like a belly, so tender, just me and the wind. I wanted Pinel to see what my song of the seas was like, how powerfully my lungs would burst forth when I was nourished only by salt air and fresh fish. And the *Santiago*, with its white sails, was at a distance, like a bride, like a best lover, like hands themselves. I remember that night. And she was beautiful, what's it matter to me; I'm speaking for Pinel, I had no illusions.

The sailors argued over cards. They were betting wine and tobacco against shirts and horses. One of them bet his allotment of Indians on a house in Madrid and lost gladly, and I fell into the same trap, losing my mule. It seems to me that those sailors had the devil himself in their wrists, and the craft and wile to save their high cards. Against a good helmet I managed to win myself a jug by drawing the high card, and I sprawled on a dune to get drunk. The soldiers asked Don Pedro to say a few words to us, but the governor turned aloof and said he would do it the next day, when the ship's stores had been loaded. That quiet way of Don Pedro's made him seem congenial even to us. Perhaps we were just too drunk to see through his intention. It makes me feel like I'm squeezing the blade of a knife when I recall the smile and measured words he bore that night. He even embraced Pinel when he saw him at his knees, almost crying. It would be better if we just didn't talk about it.

This time we went to bed early. Remember that on the eve of our departure the lads had lived it up, and that on the ride to Valparaíso they had driven the animals so hard they had raised sparks. Before saying my prayers I took the saddle off my mule and asked the new owner to treat him well. Then I looked for a rock where I could sit down to think. I thought about my dead friends, about their faces soiled by dirt and blood, with their tongues squashed over their teeth, and those turbulent eyes that made them look so horrible. I thought about those in agony who preferred to get up from their beds to defecate and urinate angrily on American soil, and to vomit it up, and to press their wounds, plunging their hands into their gashes as if trying to snatch out the crimson death that invaded them so quickly. I thought about the two rings and last three letters I was keeping in my pack (the one for Andalucía, the other for Medinaceli, and the last for the daughter in Madrid). I might have to travel over the whole country to keep my word to the dead. That's what I was thinking about on the dune when sleep overcame me so peacefully.

Perhaps I was the last to awaken. The rafts were already approaching the vessel and the men were repairing and caulking it, and I found out that Don Pedro had seen fit to order us to mint the gold aboard ship. I gave the skipper a hand with the rowing, and it took quite an effort, for we were headed windward and the wind was kicking up its heels toward the land, with Valparaíso turning to dust, and I had my feet braced against the chest holding exactly two thousand one hundred fifty pesos. Finally we put our money together in a repository on board, and for the first time we sixteen travelers were able to bear our teeth to each other smiling. I remember it because I counted three hands, and I was the missing finger. Each man, upon his bundles and suitcases, waited for the governor to come by to speak to him. But now they weren't laughing. They were silent, as if having a premonition, biting their nails, straightening the fringes on their sweaty and badly ironed shirts. Not one of them had spent a peso on breeches or doublets so as not to reduce the aid to their families in Spain. They were filthy but content.

But either it was a quirk of mine or something was in the air; or maybe it was the squawking of the birds, or the shadows the wind was folding into, or the sunlight, so yellow as it shattered on the stern rigging. I told you I'm a man of few words. I also know how to quell a hunch even though it stings like a thorn in your knee. When Don Pedro came, good old Villagra came with him, and Juan de Cárdenas, may heaven take mercy on him if he's died. The governor fluttered his hands as if they were birds trying to fly away. He touched González Marmolejo's shoulder, gave Guillermo de la Rocha a friendly punch in the belly, and he spoke more beautifully and flowery than Vicencio de Monte himself. When he talked about the struggles and misfortunes we had gone through together, he even got a sincere look in his eye. His hands got soft and warm like those of a priest right at the moment he asked us to look after his reputation before the king. And then, just when he had us all trembling in our hearts and arms, he made a gesture to the port side and, laughing, showed us what a great table, heaped with tasty dishes, wine and fish soup, had been prepared for us. It was to make up for those months of hunger in which our fantasies in bed were happy if we even imagined ourselves chewing on bones or pieces of leather. (Once I proposed that we sacrifice a horse, and the governor spat his answer out on the ground. For him it was as if we had wanted to eat our armor and swords.)

Anyway, that's how we packed the boats. In the sky the clouds had broken up and the sun was streaming down evenly everywhere, gilding the coastal sand, and flushing the soft skin of the scriveners. I withstood it happily; I may have had the toughest skin among the conquistadors, except for Bartolomé Díaz. (If that morning Bartolomé had had daggers and knives instead of a tongue and teeth, the bodies of Valdivia and Cárdenas would have ended up pinned like some repugnant shellfish on the edge of the beach.) Today we can talk calmly, isn't that right? And your ear is my friend. That's why I'll hold my temper and tell you peacefully: Díaz was honest; he said what he knew and that's the way it's written in the books.

They say that trumpeters have stomachs as deep as

hell itself, and that ballads and dances were invented by the devil himself, in Salamanca. Well, I can adore a banquet table as much as I do my mother. Better still if there are fish and loaves of bread that miraculously grow plentiful. Someone talked of composing a panegyric to Don Pedro, and there was an overflow of fraternal gestures, and there was no one who didn't gravely nod assent. I forgot about my presentiments, sucking on lampreys, tuna and hake. To get the bad taste out of my mouth, as they say, I went for the bottom of the jugs, lined up the empty bottles and was the first in smashing them on the rocks of the American shore. The men of the ship could really pack it in, and if there was no silence it was because they swore with their cheeks stuffed. At midday the governor appeared and, with his eyes on his boots, accepted the toast we had prepared for him. We all stood up, and after emptying our bottles, someone blew his nose, and we almost all had to grind dirt into our palms. That's the way we were toward that man, at that moment, that moment I would like to puke out of my memory, father. Don Pedro took off his helmet, and the sunlight entangled on his chest and in his hair. We were quiet, watching him, and he watched us watch him. Then he went very calmly to the beach, like someone who doesn't want anyone to see his tears. We bowed our heads and delicately finished off the last swallow.

It was Guillermo de Rocha who suddenly shoved back his chair and smashed his fists against the table. Pinel put his hands together as if he were praying. Hernando Vallejo squeezed his fists and bit his knuckles. We were all immobile seeing what was happening. The governor had changed his nostalgic

stride and his rush now was that of a scared woman,
of turbulent water, of a coward, looking back and
getting into the boat that had already taken to the
oars.

That's how they stole our gold, Captain Sir.
Without pity and not like men. Nothing mattered, not
our daughters, not our mothers, not our five years of
solitary labor, not honor, not even the dignity of their
own names. I thought I would drown in my own rage.
The men disbanded along the sand and shouted at the
governor to take pity on them. Pinel stayed by the
table, and was speaking in a low voice, as if Don
Pedro could hear him. He brandished arguments, and
stretched out his arms to kiss his hands. Finally Marín
managed to jump into the water, and caught up to the
boat, swimming. He tried to climb into it, and one of
the crew broke an oar over his head, and they left him
floating there. Desperate, he stroked his way back to
the beach moaning and gushing blood. We all stayed
on the shore, and when Don Pedro made his
approach to the ship, as we stood naked, crying, with
the water up to our waist; then we began to laugh, as
if we couldn't believe the laughter, as if it were all just
a bad dream, a mistake of the stars, like a joke played
by the light that was starting to lose its shadow and
was getting stiff as a knife and burned our ears. Then,
Captain Sir, this is what your grace wants me to tell
you, I climbed up on a group of nearby rocks, and
with one swipe of my fist I snatched up my trumpet,
and burning my lips on the blistering bronze of the
mouthpiece, I made it howl, splitting my teeth, like a
dog in heat, like a mountain lion, like the most
afflicted beast in the world, to the tune of that ballad
that everyone used to sing, the one that has those

words you'll remember: *watch, watch where the wolf is going, Juanica.* Eighty thousand gold pieces was what the governor reaped. In short order we will be people of no importance at all: an aged scrivener, a disillusioned trumpeter, a dropsied man stinking of manure and mud, a few merchants. Then, so that Valdivia's success would be complete, so that there would be absolutely nothing left in the bluish curve of space, I stopped blowing, and broke my trumpet into two pieces of bronze. Naked, on foot, disgusted, sweaty, just as if we had been robbed by Frenchmen, we started off walking toward Santiago.

And in a week the gallows gobbled up many heads. Pero Sancho's was privileged; they put it out to dry on a stake in the plaza. As far as I'm concerned, everything was perfect. Maybe the only bad thing was that one foggy morning in Luis de Cartagena's home, Pinel hanged himself.

"But you, Torres, made no declaration against the governor at any trial."

The trumpeter plucked the E string on the guitar.

"It's just that I never had any illusions, Captain. That's why."

About the translators:

Donald L. Schmidt is Associate Professor of Spanish at the University of Colorado at Denver. His previously published translations include short works by Antonio Skármeta, José Agustín and Augusto Salazar Bondy. He co-edited *José Agustín: Onda and Beyond* (1986) and has published articles on Spanish American narrative and drama.

Born in Chile, Federico Cordovez Anwandter holds Masters degrees in Literature from the University of Chile, and in Latin American Literature from the University of Colorado, Boulder. He has also studied under Allen Ginsberg, at the NAROPA Institute, and currently teaches Spanish at the University of Colorado at Denver.